R

MW00366667

Also by Hank Edwards

THE JUDGE

Published by
HarperPaperbacks

aw

HANK EDWARDS

THE JUDGE

WAR CLOUDS

HarperPaperbacks
A Division of HarperCollinsPublishers

HarperPaperbacks   *A Division of* HarperCollins*Publishers*
                    10 East 53rd Street, New York, N.Y. 10022

Cover illustration by Darrell Sweet

First printing: January 1991

Printed in the United States of America

HarperPaperbacks and colophon are trademarks of
HarperCollins*Publishers*

10 9 8 7 6 5 4 3 2 1

CHAPTER 1

"IF THEY'RE GOING TO HAVE AN INDIAN WAR," mused Clay Torn, "at least they have good weather for it."

It was the kind of autumn morning men dreamed about, especially in this southern part of Dakota. It was clear and crisp, with the smell of dew-wet grass heavy on the air. The low hills stood sharp against a brilliant blue sky. Hardwoods blazed orange and yellow among the deeper green of lodgepole pine. The stream, along whose valley Torn traveled, sparkled in the sun.

Torn rode easily, his tall form slouched to one side. He wore a buckskin jacket and his hat was pulled low over his eyes. A Havana cigar, freshly lit, dangled from his mouth. His horse was a sturdy roan, rented in Vermillion. He led a pack horse, in whose load were his extra clothes and the few books on Indian law and treaties that he'd been able to scare up before hurrying here from Nebraska.

Torn was headed for the Red Hills Indian Agency. An emergency summons from Attorney General George Williams had brought him from his circuit rounds to the south. The white population of Dakota was in an uproar. The reservation Indians—Northern Cheyenne—were accused of being off their grounds. Prompted by the local army commander, a major named Darcy, the whites had filed suit to have the Indians placed in default of their treaty and moved off the reservation. The attorney general had sent Torn to make a ruling.

There was a movement to Torn's right. A party of men crested a distant slope. Torn could tell they were soldiers from the way they rode. Major Darcy's battalion of cavalry was stationed at Fort Connor, near the reservation. These soldiers must be from there.

Torn halted while the troopers rode down to him. It was a standard detail, an officer and ten men. They halted a little ways off, and the officer trotted over to Torn. The officer was young, with a jaunty moustache. Beneath his uniform jacket was a plaid shirt. His battered campaign hat was turned at a rakish angle and he wore a silver bar on each shoulder.

The young officer reined in. "Good morning, sir," he said, saluting. "Lieutenant James McIntyre, Seventh Cavalry, out of Fort Connor."

Torn puffed his cigar. "Morning, lieutenant. Pleased to meet you. The name's Clay Torn." He extended a hand, and the lieutenant took it.

"Judge Torn?" the lieutenant said.

"That's right."

The lieutenant let out his breath. "Thank God you're finally here, sir."

"This isn't the easiest place to get to, son. I've ridden on everything but a hot air balloon since I left Nebraska, and I wouldn't doubt the balloon's next. Have the Indians been off the reservation again?"

"It's been quiet the last few days, but it's the quiet before the storm. This territory is a powder keg, and the fuse is mighty short."

"Both sides spoiling for a fight?"

"Yes, sir. At first, it was buffalo the Indians went after, and you couldn't blame them, the way they've been forced to live. Then they started raiding stock—horses and cattle. Everyone figures they'll go hunting scalps next. And if they do that, there's no telling what will happen. The white folks around here are armed, and they want those Cheyenne off the reservation. If the government won't do it for them, they're prepared to do it themselves. You'll have to do something quick."

Torn puffed the cigar again. "At the University of Virginia I learned that haste is not the mark of a gentleman," he said. "I'll hear all the facts before I decide whether the treaty's been broken."

The lieutenant raised an eyebrow. "Some folks will be unhappy to hear you say that, sir."

Torn didn't care. "Some folks I enjoy making unhappy."

"Are you on your way to Pine City now?"

"No. I thought I'd go to the Agency first."

"I wouldn't, sir. It's too dangerous to travel onto the reservation without an escort right now."

"Can't you be my escort?" Torn asked.

McIntyre shook his head. "Orders, sir. Our mission is to patrol the reservation boundaries. We're to try and intercept any Indians breaking out—and to keep any whites from breaking in. We're not to enter the reservation grounds under any circumstances. Major Darcy doesn't want it to look like we're trying to start an Indian war."

"And are you?"

The lieutenant stiffened. "I resent that, Judge Torn."

"Relax, son. No offense intended. Just curious to see what you'd say."

Torn pulled another cigar from his buckskin jacket. It was his last Havana, but he could always get more, and this kid lieutenant probably hadn't seen anything this good in six months or a year. "Have one?" he asked.

The lieutenant smiled broadly. "Yes, sir. I will, sir. Thank you."

Lt. McIntyre took the cigar. He lit it, savoring the aroma. He was about twenty-four. He probably had three or four years out here, with assorted skirmishes and chases, in the blistering heat of summer and bitter cold of winter, and probably at least one wound to show for it. A seasoned veteran. Well, so had Torn been, at that age. Behind the lieutenant, his detail waited patiently. They were like soldiers anywhere—the veterans businesslike, the kids scared and trying to look tough. Their uniforms were every imaginable shade of blue, and there seemed to be as many different kinds of hats as there were men.

Torn looked at the surrounding hills. "Pretty country," he remarked. "I wonder if the Cheyenne realize how lucky they are not to have lost it to the white man yet? Standing Deer is still the principal chief of the Northern Cheyenne, isn't he?"

McIntyre nodded, puffing his cigar, trying to look mature.

Torn said, "He gave you boys fits in the bad old days, didn't he?"

"Mm. Frankly, the War Department is worried that he'll break out and do it again. We're to keep *him* contained at all costs." The lieutenant straightened in the saddle. "I hate to break this off, Judge Torn, but I must continue my patrol. Are you determined to go on alone?"

Torn grinned. "It's the way I like to work."

The lieutenant grinned back. Then he saluted smartly. "Very well. Be careful, then, and good luck." He wheeled his chestnut gelding and cantered off to rejoin his men. Looking back over his shoulder, he shouted, "And thanks for the cigar!"

The soldiers rode on. Torn continued northwest, along the stream. The miles dropped away. He must be well onto the reservation now. It grew hot. He took off his buckskin jacket and tied it behind his cantle. The cigar was a cold stub in his mouth. He smelled sun-dried grass, the scent of pine.

He stopped to let his horses drink. Holding their leads, he knelt beside the stream. He splashed the cold mountain water on his face, washing off the trail dirt. He cupped his hand, and drank.

From behind him came a gunshot. A bullet kicked dust at his feet. There was another shot. He didn't see where that bullet went, and he didn't stay around to find out. He grabbed the roan's reins and vaulted into the saddle. The hell with the pack horse.

"Let's get out of here," he said.

As he dug his spurs into the roan's flanks, there were yells from the wooded hills. A file of elaborately feathered Indians charged out, waving rifles and bows.

Torn put his head low on the horse's neck. His cigar had fallen out somewhere. He threw a look over his shoulder. The loose pack horse had not slowed the Indians at all. This was a war party.

A bullet hummed by Torn's head. Another, just as close. These Indians were good shots. Torn raced along the flat land beside the creek, heading up-stream toward the Agency. There would be white men there—if any white men were still alive. He had no choice. That army patrol was half a day's ride back. He'd never reach them.

He thought about turning into the pines and forting up. No. There were too many Indians, and they were so close he wouldn't have time to dig in, or even do much more than get off his horse, before he was overwhelmed.

More shots, at least one of which came from a new Winchester. Torn couldn't see the Indians well through their dust and the dust of his own horse.

The stream looped in front of him. Torn splashed across it. Running full out, his horse slipped and stumbled on the wet rocks of the stream bottom.

"Don't lose it here," Torn shouted at the terrified animal.

On the other side of the stream, Torn galloped into a wide bend, looking down the valley anxiously, hoping for sight of white men. Hoping for a miracle.

The valley was empty.

Torn swallowed his disappointment. He swallowed his fear. The Indians drew closer. Torn prayed that one of their shots did not hit his horse, but he knew that he was just postponing the inevitable. The Indians were gaining.

Torn put his hand on his Colt pistol. It was loaded. At his belt, his saber-knife—the one made from the sword with which he killed Sgt. Karl Schmidt at Point Lookout Prison—was sharpened to a razor's edge. If it came to that.

Down the valley they rode, Torn and the Indians. The Indians weren't yelling much now. Probably they had all they could do to keep riding. Torn drew the revolver. They'd be close enough for him to use it in a minute. After that, it was just a matter of time.

The drumming of the Indians' horses was loud in Torn's ears. His thumb loosened the hammer of the Colt.

Then, from behind a wooded spur ahead of him, there was dust.

Torn's heart leaped. He held his head lower on the horse's neck. He dug in his heels, urging the roan to one last furious burst of energy. Then he saw the riders through the dust, and he brought the horse sliding to a halt, neighing and bucking in painful protest.

The riders were Indians.

CHAPTER 2

TORN LOOKED AROUND DESPERATELY. THERE was nowhere for him to go. Both ends of the valley were blocked. There were wooded hills on either side, but the Indians would be on him before he got that far.

Torn jumped off the roan. He drew his carbine from its scabbard. He cocked his pistol and put it to the horse's head, ready to make some cover for a stand.

Then he stopped. The first group of Indians had turned their horses. They were riding away, back down the valley.

The second group of Indians, the ones who had appeared from behind the spur of the hill, had halted some distance off. There were about a dozen of them. Unlike the first group, these wore no paint or feathers. Most had on at least one item of white man's clothing. Even at this distance, Torn could see that their horses were not the best. One of these Indians detached himself from the others and trotted forward. He was unarmed.

The Indian was impressive, or he had been once. He had a round, flat face and almond eyes. His jawline had grown fleshy, and there was a thickening around his waist caused by inactivity. He wore a breechclout and leggings. He was bare-chested, save for an enormous gold medal which hung from his neck. His horse's ribs showed. There was a look about the Indian, though—commanding, fearless. Torn would not want to be caught down the wrong end of this man's gunsights.

The Indian rode to where Torn stood behind the roan. Torn suspected some kind of trap, and his thumb rubbed the pistol's hammer nervously.

The Indian sat his horse in front of Torn. His imperious brown eyes met Torn's blue ones. Then the Indian quirted his horse and galloped away. When he reached his companions, he shouted, and the whole party rode off, leaving Torn by himself.

Torn breathed low. He put his guns away. He blew on his fingertips, which had gone cold. He was alone in the valley. He walked his horse a while, to let the animal cool down, then he remounted and continued on his way.

It was late afternoon when Torn arrived at the Red Hills Agency. There was a chill in the air now, and he had put his buckskin jacket back on. The Agency buildings were situated beside a pleasant stream, with long grass for grazing. In the fading sunlight, the cottonwoods and oaks blazed with autumn color. Across the stream, the model farm looked unattended. A sparse corn crop had been grown, but it had gone unharvested and been allowed to decay.

The Agency was quiet; there was no one visible. The buildings were shut tight, and there were a few horses in the corral. A wisp of smoke curled from the main building's chimney.

The main door opened as Torn approached. Two army officers stepped out, followed by two other men. All carried rifles, and they were wary, as if expecting to be attacked. The four men blinked, as their eyes adjusted to the fading sunlight.

"Afternoon, gents," Torn said. He fought his instinctive dislike of the blue uniform; it had represented the enemy for so long. The first officer was a major. Everything about him said "cavalry," from his tight jacket and trousers, to his gleaming high boots, to his kepi with havelock, tilted over one eye. His moustache was immaculately waxed and trimmed. The top buttons of his tunic were open, allowing a yellow silk scarf to show. The other officer was a captain, dressed in an old blue coat and slouch hat.

The major said, "You're a cool one, to ride in this way. Don't you know we're under siege here?"

"No," Torn said. "How long's it been going on?"

"Since yesterday," said one of the civilians, a bearded fellow with a dirty shirt and a flushed face. "Standing Deer and his people moved their camp deep into the reservation. Then they ran off all the

Agency stock. We haven't seen an Indian since, but they're out there. I can feel it."

"You're right about that part," Torn said. "I just got jumped by a war party."

Only the captain seemed surprised. "What happened?" said the second civilian. He was a pale, slender fellow, with a high, domed forehead, thin lips, and a beaked nose, which made him look rather like a self-righteous sparrow. He wore fringed buckskin shirt and pants, and two revolvers with the butts reversed. In his thin hands was a Sharps .50 rifle.

Torn got off his horse. While he led the animal into the corral, he told the men about the attack.

"How did you get away?" asked the bird-faced civilian.

"I got saved by another bunch of Indians."

The four men looked at each other, puzzled. The man with the flushed face said, "I can't think who that might have been. I can't think of a single Cheyenne on this reservation who would help a white man right now."

"Who are you, anyway?" queried the bird-faced fellow.

"I'm Clayton R. Torn, judge of the U.S. Circuit Court."

The bird-faced fellow raised his shaggy eyebrows. "So you're Clay Torn. I must say, you don't look like a judge." He held out a hand, "I'm Cyrus Van Horne, of the House Committee on Indian Affairs."

Van Horne's well-manicured hand was lost in Clay's big paw. "I know you by reputation, congressman," Clay said. He should have. Van Horne

was one of those who, years before, had led the fight
to block Clay's nomination to the Federal bench.

Van Horne smiled. "Yes, I suppose you do. You'll
also know that you don't get far in politics by holding
grudges. Yesterday's enemy is tomorrow's friend.
The past is past, eh?"

"If you say so, Congressman. What are you doing
here?"

"I've come to investigate conditions on this reservation. I've received numerous complaints about
the outbreaks here, and I want to see for myself."
He indicated the army officers, "This is Major Darcy
and Captain Harman, of the Seventh Cavalry.
They're here as official observers."

Darcy nodded curtly. Something about Torn did
not seem to sit well with him. The captain shook
Torn's hand. Congressman Van Horne turned to the
man with the flushed face. "This is Amos Larrabee,
agent for Red Hills."

Torn shook Larrabee's hand; it was sweaty, nervous. The Indian agent was unsteady on his feet, as
if he'd been drinking.

Larrabee said, "You can bunk in the Agency building with the rest of us, Judge. Hope you don't mind
taking your turn at corral guard?"

"Not at all," Torn said.

Torn unsaddled his horse and rubbed him down.
Congressman Van Horne said, "You see the gravity
of the situation here, Judge. You yourself have been
attacked."

Major Darcy added, "If we act now, we can surprise the Indians, before Standing Deer leads them
off the reservation, and they escape into the Bad-

lands. We'll give Standing Deer the thrashing he deserves—pay him back for what he's done to us over the years."

Larrabee looked at him. "I . . . I thought you were just going to relocate the Indians, Major. I don't want blood on my hands."

Van Horne and the major paid the Indian agent no heed. Van Horne said, "Perhaps we can consider the war to have begun. After all, Standing Deer attacked the judge."

Darcy shook his head. "No. There's too many reporters around, ready to take the Indians' side. We need a clear provocation."

"You mean we need an innocent person killed?" asked Van Horne.

"That, or an attack on the Agency," Darcy said.

Torn said, "Seems to me you're inviting an attack, if it's as dangerous as you say. Why don't you have troops here?"

Major Darcy laughed ruefully. "Under terms of our treaty with the Cheyenne, no more than two officers are allowed on the reservation at any time, and no troops. We obey the treaty to the letter. That way, when it's broken, those Eastern do-gooders can't blame the army."

Torn watered his horse, then turned him out in the corral. He walked to the Agency building, escorted by the four men. The western sky was turning red. Fallen leaves blew across their path.

It was warmer inside the building. There was stew bubbling in a pot over the fire. Whatever the food was, it didn't have much aroma. "Salt beef and dessicated vegetables," Larrabee said apologetically.

"Since the stock's been run off, that's what we're down to."

"Make yourself at home, Judge," said Congressman Van Horne, putting down his rifle. He pointed to a table with several bottles and glasses. "You look like you could use a drink."

"I could use two or three of them," Torn said. "I thought my number was up back there."

Larrabee said, "You're lucky it wasn't up, if Standing Deer was after you. Standing Deer's problem is that he can't forget the old ways. He thinks his people should be free to raid and hunt as they please. It's a new world, and he can't adjust to it."

"None of them can," said Major Darcy.

"Standing Deer is a menace to honest men everywhere," said Van Horne. "The sooner he's put where he can't hurt anyone, the better."

Torn poured a couple fingers of whiskey into the glass and slugged it down. "Scotch," he said appreciatively. "You bring expensive provisions into the wilderness, Congressman."

Torn poured again. This time he sipped it. "What you all say may be true, but I've found that it pays to hear both sides of a story."

"Meaning?" said Darcy.

"Meaning, I want to hear what the Indians have to say. I want to talk to Standing Deer."

"Oh, for Christ's sake," said Darcy. Van Horne looked disgusted.

Torn put down the glass. He faced the four men. "Understand me, gentlemen. I am a Federal judge. I am sworn to be impartial, and I don't give my oath lightly. I intend to hold a council the day after tomorrow, at Council Butte. I'll invite white men and Indians, and I'll learn the facts of this case. Then, and only then, will I give my decision."

Only Captain Harman, who was keeping watch at the window, seemed to approve of Torn's words. Larrabee, the Indian Agent, said, "You'll never get close enough to Standing Deer to invite him. He won't come to the Agency. He hasn't been here since it was built. To him we don't exist. He sends his son if he has business with the whites. The only way to talk to Standing Deer is to go to his camp."

"Then that's what I'll do," Torn said.

"You can't!" said Van Horne. "This country's swarming with hostiles. It's certain death out there."

"I'll take my chances," Torn told him.

"Standing Deer's camp is deep in the Red Hills," Larrabee said. "You'll never find it by yourself, and I guarantee I'll not go with you."

"I'll go with you." It was Captain Harman, from his post at the window.

The captain looked at Major Darcy. "Standing Deer knows me, sir. He trusts me, if he trusts any white man. I know approximately where his camp is. I've been out there before."

Darcy shook his head. "I can't authorize you to commit suicide, captain."

Harman pressed on, "It's worth a try, sir, if it'll prevent a war."

Darcy plainly didn't agree, but at last he said, "Very well, Captain. You may escort the judge to Standing Deer's camp."

"Thank you, sir," Harman said. To Torn, he said, "We'll leave at first light."

"Does Standing Deer speak English?" Torn asked.

"Yes," answered Larrabee. "He was quite friendly with the whites at one time. Then something went wrong with him."

Captain Harman snorted. "What went wrong was that some settler shot his oldest son for target practice."

Larrabee dished out dinner soon after—stew and stale bread to soak in it. While the men took their seats, Torn hung his jacket and gunbelt on a wall peg. Major Darcy saw Torn's dagger on the gunbelt.

"An unusual weapon, Judge. May I look at it?"

"Suit yourself," Torn told him.

The major took the knife from its hand-made sheath. He ran a finger along the polished blade. "Where did you get this?"

"I made it."

"Excellent work. It's a cavalry saber, isn't it? The 1861 army issue. Your accent says you're Sesesh, Judge. How'd you come by this?"

Torn didn't want to talk about it. "It's a long story."

Major Darcy kept prodding. "How'd a Sesesh become a judge, anyway? I thought your sort were barred from Federal office."

"I guess you thought wrong, Major," Torn said.

Darcy returned the saber-knife to its sheath. He laughed condescendingly. "You know, I fought all through the war, and I don't think I saw one man killed by a sword."

Torn made no reply. He had an idea that he would have enough trouble on his hands tomorrow. There was no sense courting more right now.

CHAPTER 3

TORN AND CAPTAIN HARMAN RODE OUT JUST after breakfast. It was another beautiful day. The few wispy clouds only accented the stunning blue of the sky.

Torn wore his buckskin jacket, the captain his old coat and slouch hat. Captain Harman was of medium height, compactly built. He had short blond hair and a blond moustache. The seat and inside legs of his uniform trousers were reinforced with buckskin, and he carried his revolver in an open holster, like a cowboy.

Their wary eyes searched the low hills as they rode. The captain said, "Council Butte—you picked a good spot for your hearing. You must know this country."

"A little," Torn said.

"Do you enjoy your work? Being a judge, I mean. It seems like it would get boring—reading law briefs, and all."

"Sometimes there's a bit of excitement," Torn said. "Anyway, what could be more boring than reading army regulations?"

The captain laughed.

"You like the army?" Torn inquired.

Harman laughed again. "There's times I wonder. Like now."

Torn said, "Major Darcy didn't want you coming with me, did he?"

"I don't care," Harman said. "I don't want another Indian war. Those poor people have suffered enough. We're not fighting the Indians, we're exterminating them."

"Darcy wouldn't think you're on the right side," Torn said.

Harman looked over at him. "Let me tell you something, Judge. We in the army may fight Indians, but it doesn't mean we enjoy it. A lot of my boys think the Indians are getting the short end of the stick. But we're professionals. We do what we're told."

"What's your view of the situation here?"

"Your guess is as good as mine," Harman said. "I've just returned to the regiment. I've been recovering from wounds I got last year. All the evidence indicates the Indians are ready for the warpath again. But Standing Deer is a man of his word. He wouldn't break the treaty unless he was convinced we'd broken it first."

The captain worked out a kink in his neck. "I'll tell you the truth, Judge, everything's changed since I was last here. Larrabee used to be the reservation trader, now he's the Indian Agent. He used to be a friend of the Indians—hell, he's got a Cheyenne wife—now he's talking war against them. Plus, you've got this grandstanding congressman, and Jim Murtaugh buying everything that's not nailed down."

"Who's Jim Murtaugh?" Torn said.

"A land speculator—a developer, he calls himself. He owns half of Pine City. That's what I mean about change—six months ago, Pine City wasn't even here."

"Why's it here now?"

"It's a boomtown, a staging point for potential settlers. There must be a thousand men there, all gambling that the Indians will be run off the reservation, and the land opened for settlement."

The land turned rough. The Red Hills rose before them, a giant citadel of rock and lodgepole pine. "These hills cover an area as big as the state of Rhode Island," Harman told Torn. "You could look for Standing Deer a long time in here and not find him. They get their name from the red soil. It reminds me a lot of Georgia."

There was red clay in South Carolina, too, and Harman's words made Torn think of home, and Melony, and things that happened a long time ago.

The two men entered the hills. They rode through a fantastic maze of hills and towering rock, of pine woods and twisting canyons. Harman led them down a narrow valley. Their horses hoofs crunched the rocky ground. No birds sang. No animals chattered.

"Is it always this quiet?" Torn asked.

"Not always," said the captain.

As if in answer to their thoughts, files of Indians rode out of the woods on either side of them.

Harman curbed his nervous horse. He and Torn continued on. The Indians rode parallel to the two white men. The Indians wore no paint or feathers, but they carried weapons. Some had bows, others had rifles or pistols.

"I thought Indians weren't supposed to have fire-arms," Torn said.

Harman said, "They must have hidden them some-where at the surrender, then dug them up. They're ready for war, all right. All they need is to put on the paint."

Suddenly the narrow valley opened. Before the two men was a broad expanse of prairie, tucked among the hills. On the prairie was the great circle camp of the Northern Cheyenne.

The two white men rode into the camp through its eastern opening, followed by their escort. The whites were greeted by a strange quiet. Old men and women stared from under thin, moth-eaten robes. Young men, who should have been out hunt-ing, sat sullenly by their campfires. Naked children watched the visitors, wide-eyed. The Indians were emaciated, starving. Bones showed through the bare chests of the men. The stomachs of the infants and children protruded from malnutrition. Women and girls listlessly pounded bowls of nuts and berries. There was hatred in every eye.

At this time of year, there should have been racks of buffalo meat drying in front of the lodges. There were none. Torn noticed that many of the tipis were blue or blue striped. He fought his reluctant horse close to one of them. Ignoring the hostile gaze of an old Cheyenne woman, he leaned from the saddle and touched the tipi. It was made of cheap cotton quilt. He gave Harman a disbelieving look.

"Government issue," the soldier explained. "There's no more buffalo for hides."

Torn could imagine how much protection the flimsy cotton tipi would provide when wet, or sagging under a load of snow, or bent by the bitter winter winds. A chill ran through him.

Harman seemed to know what he was thinking, for he said, "They tell me that two out of every ten Indians on the reservation died last winter. This winter figures to be worse. This winter, they won't have their dogs and horses to eat."

Then Torn knew what it was about this camp that had struck him as odd. There were no barking dogs.

"They ate their animals?" he said.

"It was that, or starve," Harman told him.

"What about the rations the government was supposed to provide for them?"

Harman shrugged. "Larrabee says they were delivered. Like I said, I wasn't here."

From the far side of the camp, a horseman approached. The horseman was naked to the waist, and he carried a feathered war lance. Torn and Harman reined in.

"It's Gray Thunder," Harman said. "Standing Deer's son-in-law."

The Indian wheeled his mount before them, and as he did, he threw the lance into the ground. The white men's horses reared. The feathers on the lance fluttered in the breeze. The dust blew away slowly.

The Indian looked at them with a contorted face. There was a scar under his lip. His scalp lock was long, almost to his waist. "What do you want here?" he demanded.

"We have come to speak to Standing Deer," Torn said.

"Why?"

"We wish to prevent the trouble that is coming."

"You can prevent nothing," the Indian said. "The trouble will come whether you wish it or not. Go, while you are able. Or let the war begin now."

"Wait," said a voice.

Torn and Harman turned. A tall, impressive young Indian strode across the camp ground. The others stepped aside to let him pass.

The young Indian was handsome and dignified. His movements were fluid, silky. Like most Cheyenne, he had no well-defined musculature. He wore a bear claw necklace and a white man's blue flannel shirt, along with his breech clout and leggings. His braids were bound with wolf fur. He pulled the lance from the ground and handed it to Gray Thunder. "These white men have come in peace, Gray Thunder. They are guests. We must not violate the laws of hospitality."

"*They* violate the laws of hospitality quickly enough," said Gray Thunder. "Do you not remember your own sister, Fawn, killed by the white soldiers when they attacked our camp on Sand Creek?"

"Those were different white men," said the young Indian.

"In the end, all white men are the same. They all want to take away our freedom."

The young Indian had no reply for that. He turned to the white men. "Greetings, Harman. It is good to see you again."

"Greetings, Runs With the Wind," said the soldier. "It is good to see you. I have brought a friend. He has come many miles to see your father. He brings word of peace."

Runs With the Wind shook his head. "He should have brought such words sooner. It is too late, now."

"Please," Torn said. "I have seen enough killing in my time. Too much killing. I do not wish to see more."

Runs With the Wind considered. At last, he said. "Very well. I will take you to my father."

"Bah!" cried Gray Thunder. "You have not changed, Runs With the Wind. You are still the white man's lackey. You are not a warrior, like your father. I say, kill them now." Torn heard agreement from the Indians in the background.

Runs With the Wind ignored them. To the white men, he said, "Leave your horses here. My people will look after them."

Torn and Harman dismounted. They followed Runs With the Wind across the camp circle. Gray Thunder stalked behind. They headed toward a red-painted lodge, and Harman said, "Your father is not with the hunters today?"

"Why should he hunt?" said Runs With the Wind. "There is no more game. The buffalo are gone from the Red Hills. They will not come back."

Behind them, the other Cheyenne pressed closer.

There was movement. The Indians were concealing things beneath their blankets. Torn caught a gleam of gun metal. He tried not to look scared. Beside him, he felt Harman tense.

They came to the red lodge. Out front, on a pole, was Standing Deer's shield, painted red, with eagle feathers bunched in the center. Runs With the Wind ducked through the lodge entrance. Torn and Harman followed, with Gray Thunder behind.

Inside, the lodge was dark. It smelled of old smoke and musty buffalo robes. Torn and Harman turned to the right, as was the Cheyenne custom. There was a shadowy figure seated in the lodge's rear. The white men joined Runs With the Wind, and they sat, crosslegged, at the figure's left. Runs With the Wind said something to his father in the Cheyenne tongue. As Torn's eyes grew accustomed to the darkness, he saw the chief more clearly, and he started.

It was the Indian who had saved him from the war party.

Standing Deer did not acknowledge the white men's presence. He stared, as if in a trance. His heavy features seemed to radiate wisdom and leadership. The gold medal around his neck gleamed faintly.

Torn waited for a pipe to be offered, and then realized there wasn't going to be one. It was the deepest form of insult to a visitor.

Torn cleared his throat. "Greetings, Standing Deer."

There was no answer.

Torn tried again. "I am called Clay Torn. I have come from the White Chief in Washington. He has sent me to learn if the Cheyenne have broken the treaty between our peoples."

Standing Deer acted like Torn wasn't there.

Torn went on, "The white men say that your people are thieves, Standing Deer. They say that you plan war against them. They say that Standing Deer is not a man of his word."

Torn thought he saw the old chief's back stiffen. He thought the almond eyes opened, just a bit. Then the look of impassivity returned.

Torn kept going. It was too late to stop now. "I am a fair man, Standing Deer. I have sworn an oath on it. I wish no innocent man punished, nor any guilty man to go free. I have seen things on this reservation that trouble me. I have seen things that make me ashamed of my race. I wish to help you."

"Do not listen, Father!" hissed Gray Thunder. "We have heard the white man's offers of help before."

Torn ignored the outburst. The renewed silence in the tent seemed to crackle. Torn said, "But if I am to help you, you must help me. Tornorrow, when the sun is highest, I will hold a great council, at Council Butte. You must come to this council, Standing Deer, and you must bring all your chiefs. At this council, I will listen to the white man, and I will listen to the red. I will weigh their words, and I will decide what is to be done."

There was still no acknowledgment of the white men's presence. Torn felt the hair on the back of his neck rise. Then Runs With the Wind stood. "You must leave now," he told the white men.

Torn and Harman followed the young Indian out

the open flap of the lodge. Behind them, Gray Thunder was urging something in low tones—it took no great imagination to figure out what.

Runs With the Wind took the white men's horses from the men who held them. He handed the reins to Torn and Harman. His handsome face was stern. "Go back to your Agency. Go quickly. For your sake, do not linger in these hills. Not like the others."

Torn and Captain Harman mounted. They started out of the Cheyenne camp. Torn fought down the urge to spur his horse and ride away as fast as he could.

"Who are 'the others?'" Torn asked Harman.

"I don't know," Harman said, "and I don't think this is a good time to stick around and find out. Do you think you made any impression on Standing Deer?"

"We'll find out tomorrow," replied Torn.

CHAPTER 4

PINE CITY WAS WAITING FOR A LAND RUSH.
Most people lived in tents. Tin chimneys stuck out
of dirty gray canvas. There were only a few buildings
of wood, and those were of the flimsiest make. There
was no lumber piled, no construction in progress.
No one was expecting to winter here.

The camp's rutted streets were jammed with
traffic—wagons and mule trains bringing in supplies,
settlers arriving, soldiers from the fort, reporters
and photographers looking for the war. The dust was
choking. The town smelled of manure and rotting
garbage. It smelled of animals and privies and cooking
food. The air was loud with the cries of men and
animals.

Instinctively, Torn checked the faces of the few

women, looking for Melony. She wasn't here, just as she hadn't been in the hundreds of other places Torn had visited since the South had surrendered, but he didn't let that upset him. He would keep searching.

The town's population was mostly bearded young men, wearing the rough flannel shirts and high boots of laborers. As Torn rode in, many of these men were streaming toward the town center. Torn followed, curious.

In front of a tent with the hand-painted sign "Pine City *Clarion*," was a crowd. A heavy-set man, prematurely bald, with a short beard, seemed to be in charge. Beside him was a breathless cowboy. The big man waved at the newcomers. To the cowboy he said, "Tell them what you just told the rest of us."

The cowhand repeated his news. "There's been eighteen horses stole from the McMurtry place, on Plum Creek."

There were cries of outrage. "Was it Injuns?" shouted someone.

"Oh, it was Indians, all right. I seen 'em. I followed their tracks onto the reservation, just like always."

"What's the army doing about it?" shouted another.

The big man answered. "I'll tell you what they're doing. Nothing. Just like always."

There were more cries and oaths.

The big man went on, "We all know where those horses are, don't we? They're in front of Standing Deer's lodge—unless he's riding them on another raid. What I want to know is, how much longer are we going to allow this to go on? Are we going to wait till our families are butchered by these savages before we act?"

"No!" the men shouted. "We've had enough!"

"Then get your guns. If the army won't do the job, we'll do it ourselves, the way Americans always have. We're enlisting a regiment of militia, the Pine City Volunteers. Jim Murtaugh's going to be colonel. He's offered to provide ammunition—and drinks."

There were cheers.

Clay forced his horse to the front of the crowd. "You're not going anywhere," he told the big man. He turned to the crowd. "Boys, my name is Clay Torn. I'm a judge of the U.S. Circuit Court, and I'm telling you—if any of you go onto that reservation, you'll be in violation of Federal ordinances, and you'll be prosecuted to the fullest extent of the law."

There was angry talk. The big man said, "Clay Torn—say, I heard of you. I heard you like to be judge *and* jury."

"I like to see that justice is done," Torn said. "I've been sent to clean up this Indian mess. There will be a hearing tomorrow, at Council Butte. I'll hear evidence against the Cheyenne then. In the meantime, I want you to break up this assembly. We'll have no private armies out here."

The big man protested, "Hey, militia ain't no . . . ."

"Don't talk to me about militia. You need the approval of the governor and the Congress for a proper militia. My guess is, you have neither, Mr . . . ?"

"Gallagher. Pete Gallagher."

"Well, Mr. Gallagher, the next time I catch you

trying to stir these men up, I'll swear out a warrant against you."

Gallagher grinned, revealing broken teeth. "That warrant might be hard to serve, Judge. There ain't what you'd call no duly constituted law in Pine City."

"Then I'll serve it myself," Torn told him.

There was no mistaking the look in Torn's pale eyes. Gallagher swallowed. "Mr. Murtaugh ain't gonna like this," he warned.

"Murtaugh, Murtaugh—I'm beginning not to like that name," Clay said. "Tell me, where do I find this Murtaugh?"

Gallagher motioned down the street with his thumb, "This time of day—try the Club Room."

"Thanks," Clay said.

"Don't mention it, Judge." Gallagher grinned again.

Torn left his horse at a livery stable. Then he checked in at a hotel, which was just a big cabin, where men rolled in their blankets and slept on the floor, with meals a dollar each.

After that, he was ready for the Club Room. The saloon was a frame building, with a canvas roof painted in stripes of red, white and blue. Inside, it was crowded and loud. Tobacco smoke hung in wreaths. The bar was made from warped planks balanced on whiskey barrels. There were tables for monte and faro, and business was better than Torn might have expected. Here and there, whores circulated.

Torn decided to have a drink before looking for Murtaugh. The bar might be crude, but there were a lot of bottles behind it. "Any chance you'd have

Old Signature?" he asked the barman.

The barman was a sweaty, overworked fellow, with greasy hair and a stained apron. He looked behind him and scratched his head, "I got Hermitage, and Jim Beam, and Delta King. I got champagne and scotch and about everything else you could think of, but I ain't got Old Signature. I never even heard of it. What is it, some kind of private label?"

"No, it's not private," Torn said, and for a second his eyes got a far-away look. "It was once a rather large label, but that was before the war." He sighed. "Hermitage will do."

The barman poured Torn's whiskey in a dirty glass. Torn sipped it, cutting the trail dust. It had been years since he'd found a place with Old Signature. He remembered lawn parties before the war, with the ladies' taffeta dresses rustling and the Spanish moss bending in the breeze, and his cousin Rafe down from Kentucky, making his Signature juleps.

Ah, well, he thought. Bygone days.

One corner of the saloon had been taken over by reporters, dressed in Easterners' ideas of frontier clothing—fringed gauntlets, outlandishly wide brimmed hats, corduroy hunting suits, gaiters, revolvers in shiny new holsters. They had monopolized the piano and were singing the latest music hall favorites. Torn caught snatches of their conversation:

"Did you hear? A war party was sighted at Five-Mile Station today."

"I heard it was Plum Creek. Where the horses were stolen."

"Maybe there's more than one war party."

"You don't think they'll attack the town, do you?"

"I don't know, but I'm sleeping with my rifle. I just wish I knew how to use it."

They were interrupted by a commotion down the bar, where a man and woman were having words. The man wore a black suit and string tie. He had a bullet-shaped head, heavy brows, and he looked like he was used to getting his way. The girl had full lips and a mane of golden hair, worn unfashionably loose. She said something the man didn't like. He grabbed her wrist and twisted it, bending her sideways and making her cry with pain.

A saloon girl and a well-heeled customer. It was none of Torn's business.

He went over.

"Leave her alone," he told the bullet-headed man.

The man turned. The saloon grew silent.

The bullet-headed man looked Torn up and down. "Butt out, friend. This ain't your affair."

"I'm making it my affair," Torn told him.

"Yeah?" The bullet-headed man shoved the girl into the bar; she hit it with a thump. "Then you just made a big mistake."

"Hey!" shouted somebody. "It's that Injun-loving judge."

The bullet-headed man smiled. It was not a friendly smile. "Is that so?" he said. "I heard what you said to Pete Gallagher, Judge. You stick your nose everywhere, don't you?"

"Everywhere it interests me."

The bullet-headed man indicated the girl, still wincing from her thump against the bar. "Well, what are you going to do about this? Issue a restraining order?"

There was laughter from the crowd.

"I could do that," Torn replied. "Or I could just beat the hell out of you."

The bullet-headed man grinned. His eyes opened with excitement. "Try it," he said. He took off his hat, put it with his cane on the bar. He shucked his coat and loosened his collar. He looked like a brawler, with a powerful, blocky build.

Torn took off his buckskin jacket and hat. People got out of the way.

Torn barely had time to get set, when the man came at him with a bull-like charge. Torn sidestepped him, clubbed him in the ear and sent him off balance into the crowd. The man turned and came at Torn again. He was quicker than Torn had figured. He exterted constant pressure, arms swinging. With the crowd pressed close, there was no room to back up. Torn was trapped. All he could do was cover up. Painful blows rained on his forearms and shoulders. One blow got through to his ribs and took his breath away. Another made his ears ring. He tried to push off and get some fighting room, but the bullet-headed man was all over him, grunting with the force of his punches, not seeming to tire at all. Torn managed to slide away. The two men exchanged punches. Both were rocked. They exchanged again, were rocked again, and drew off. Torn gasped for breath. There was blood from the bullet-headed man's nose, it spread fan-like across the lower portion of his face. The man smeared it off with his sleeve. He reached behind him, picked a bottle from the bar and threw it. Torn ducked. The man charged behind the bottle, head lowered. His head caught Torn in the stomach, bowling him backward. The two men crashed into a card table. Torn's spine hit the table's edge painfully. They fell to the floor, with cards and chips spilling everywhere. On the floor they grappled, amid the vomit and spilled whiskey. The man pummeled Torn. He tried to wedge himself onto Torn's chest, to sit there and beat his face in. Torn tried to get off his back, but the man was strong. The man lunged with a long fingernail, trying to dig out Torn's eyeball. Torn dodged the blow. The fingernail raked a cut alongside his eye. Torn shoved the heel of his hand under the man's jaw, snapping the man's teeth together and his head back. He did it again, and he followed it with a fingertip jab to the man's adam's apple. The man gagged. He went momentarily limp. Torn pushed him off, then tried to get to his knees, but the man recovered and lunged after him. Torn swung an elbow and caught the man's face coming in. There was a crunching sound. The man dropped to his hands. Blood dripped onto the dirt floor. Seemingly in slow motion, Torn turned on his knees, facing the man. He swung his right hand and caught the man flush on the cheek, knocking him over backwards.

Torn crawled to his feet. The bullet-headed man pulled himself up, using the bar. He reached into his coat and brought out a pistol. Torn dodged as the pistol fired. The shot went wide. The crowd shouted. Men dropped to the floor or ran. Before the bullet-headed man could fire again, Torn leaped on him. He grabbed his gun arm and smashed the wrist against the bar. The man cried out and dropped the pistol. He grappled with Torn and tried to chew off his ear. Torn threw an elbow into the man's stomach, then shouldered him into the bar, hard. Before the man could recover, Torn squared and punched him in the gut. The man doubled over. Torn held the back of the man's hair, and he swung his knee into the man's face. The man grunted and fell to the dirt floor. He didn't move.

Torn bent over, heaving for breath. His legs felt rubbery. He wanted to lay down—to fall down—but pride wouldn't let him, not in front of this crowd. His ribs ached. Blood—his own and the other man's— was all over him. One of his teeth felt loose. His shirt was torn and one knee was out of his trousers. His back hurt where he'd hit the table. It was hard to stand straight.

He realized that everyone in the saloon was talking. Many of them were talking at him. He couldn't tell what they were saying. It was all a roar. The room spun.

He took a deep breath, wishing he was outside in the fresh air. The bullet-headed man's friends had raised him to a sitting position. The man's mouth was full of blood. There was blood on his shirt and face.

One of the reporters, a gangly fellow with eye-glasses, approached Torn. "Where'd you learn to fight like that, Judge?"

"In Charleston," Clay said. He shook his fist. The knuckles were scraped bare, and they hurt like hell. He looked around. "Can somebody tell me where I can find a fellow called Jim Murtaugh?"

The bespectacled reporter cleared his throat. "Actually, that's Jim Murtaugh, there." He pointed to the bullet-headed man.

Torn swore. "We've been introduced," he said.

With the assistance of his friends, Murtaugh wobbled to his feet. Somebody tried to wipe the blood from his face with a kerchief, but Murtaugh shrugged him off. Murtaugh got his coat, hat and cane. Somebody else already had his pistol. Murtaugh looked hard at Torn. He spit blood. Then his friends helped him from the saloon.

Torn's head throbbed. He needed to get out in the fresh air. He looked for his hat.

The golden-haired girl handed it to him.

"Thanks, ma'am," Torn said.

The girl had a fresh face, with sparkling green eyes. "It's I who should be thanking you," she told him.

"Don't mention it," Torn said. He put on the hat, grimacing with pain. "Next time, find a more convivial customer, will you?"

The girl looked like she didn't understand. Then she reddened with anger. "Customer! What do you think I am, a whore?"

"Yes," Torn said. He'd heard this line a hundred times before.

"How dare you!" she said, outraged.

Torn was unimpressed. "Well, if you're not, then pardon the language, ma'am, but you should have more damn sense than to be in a saloon."

The girl looked stunned. Torn touched his hat brim. "Good evening, ma'am."

He turned away from her, and shouldered his way

out of the saloon, limping a little because his old war wound had started to hurt. Outside, he stood in the street, letting the cool air caress his face. He started to walk away.

Then behind him, he heard the girl cry, "Wait!"

CHAPTER

5

THE GOLDEN-HAIRED GIRL FOLLOWED TORN
from the saloon. Passers-by stared at Torn's battered face and ripped clothes. He didn't care.

"You look awful," the girl said. "Are you all right?"

Torn limped along. He wiggled the loose tooth
with his tongue. "I've been better."

"Are you really a Federal judge?" she asked.

"That's right," Torn said. "But if you're trying to
have a case thrown out of court, don't get your hopes
up. I don't work that way. Anyway, I'm not here to
conduct circuit rounds."

"I know why you're here," the girl said. "What I
want is an interview."

Torn stopped. "An interview?"

"For my paper, the New York *Tribune*."

Torn looked at her closely. Until this moment, he'd still figured her for a whore. "What are you, some kind of reporter?"

"Yes," she said, sounding peeved because he hadn't believed her.

"But, you're a . . . you're a girl."

Her full lips compressed into a withering smile. "That's a very astute observation, Mr. Torn. I see now why they made you a judge."

"I still don't believe it," Torn said. "The only female reporter I ever heard of was Penelope Winslow, and you can't be her."

"Why not?" she said.

"For one reason, you're too young. Penelope Winslow's been around for a while."

"Any other reason?"

Torn cleared his throat, uncomfortably. "Well, face it, Penelope Winslow leads what you might call an active love life. To hear you talk, you're still wet behind the ears."

The girl smiled smugly. "I assure you, my ears are quite dry, Judge. And I *am* Penelope Winslow. You may call me Penny, if you like."

Torn stared. Penelope Winslow was a celebrity, the heroine of her own stories. She was a reporter, but she made headlines as much by the way she gathered her stories as by their journalistic content. She had covered the Ashanti War in west Africa. She had visited Lake Albert with Samuel White Baker, and searched for the elusive missionary Livingstone along the Congo. She had traveled among cannibals in Uganda. She had fled from slave dealers in Zanzibar. Her books about her experiences had been best sellers.

They started walking again. "Tell me," Torn said skeptically. "Did you really disguise yourself as an Arab and sneak into Mecca, or was that made up for publicity?"

Penny looked resentful. "No, I really did it."

"What was it like?"

She thought for a moment. "Let's just say I wouldn't do it again," she replied at last.

Torn smiled. "What are you doing in Dakota? I thought you were in France, covering the war with Prussia."

"I became ill during the siege of Paris. I had to return home. Now that I'm better, my editors want me out here, to cover the Indian war."

"Everybody seems confident there's going to be a war," Torn said.

Penny laughed. "If there isn't one, a lot of people are going to be disappointed."

"That's a cynical attitude."

"You get cynical in this business. On my last assignment, I saw Parisians eat the animals in their zoo. I saw them eat each other. That's not the sort of thing to make you optimistic about the human condition. And let's be realistic—peace doesn't sell papers. The flower of the American press are here. They're falling all over themselves, trying to get the *big* story."

"Which, of course, you intend to get first."

Penny's green eyes twinkled. "Of course."

"Which is why you want that interview."

"Right again."

"I'm flattered, Miss Winslow, but the answer is no. I have nothing to say to you—on or off the record."

Torn started walking again. Penny ran to catch up. "Come on, Judge. You and I could help each other. There're things I've learned that might interest you."

Torn turned on her. "Like what?"

"Do I get the interview?" she said.

"Depends on what you've got."

That seemed good enough for Penny. She said, "Doesn't it seem odd to you that all these unemployed men here have money for drinking and gambling?"

"I had wondered about that," Torn said.

"Well, it's because they're not unemployed. At least seven hundred of them are drawing weekly wages from the Prometheus Company."

"Who, or what, is the Prometheus Company?" Torn asked.

"I don't know. They have an office in town, but they're tight with information."

"Is Murtaugh involved with them?"

"Murtaugh won't talk about his business dealings. It's policy with him. No one knows what he's really worth, or how many pies he's got his fingers in. He's a fascinating character, in a way. You know he started as a prospector?"

"I can believe it," Torn said. "He's got the look."

"He was in California during the Gold Rush. He was just a boy then, but he must have done all right. He's been going strong ever since."

"How did you get involved with him?" Torn said.

"I asked him for an interview," Penny said. She
shook her head, "He thought I was after something
else. Really, the ego of that man. I've been propo-
sitioned by everyone from a pirate king to a real
king. A headhunter offered to make me his seventh
wife. But I've never encountered anyone quite so
crude as Mr. Murtaugh."

She brightened. "There, I've told you what I have.
Now, about that interview. When do I get it?"

"You don't," Torn told her.

Her eyes opened wide. Her mouth quivered in
anger. "That's not fair! I gave you the information
about the Prometheus Company. You have to give
me something in return."

"No, I don't," Torn said. "To me, you're just a
concerned citizen, coming forward and trying to
help." He tipped his hat to her. "Good evening, Miss
Winslow."

He left her in the crowded street, fuming.

Torn went for a bath and a shave. The hot water
felt good on his cuts and bruises. Then he bought
an off-the-shelf black suit, to replace the one he'd
lost with the pack horse and make him look properly
judicial for tomorrow. The suit was made for a man
twenty pounds lighter and four inches shorter, but
it was the best one he could find, and he paid for it
with his own funds. The government only allowed
him mileage and meal money.

Next, he stopped at the Ritz restaurant, on the
main street. Inside, he sat at a crowded trestle table.
He ordered a beefsteak, a potato, and fried onions,
along with a glass of beer to wash them down. The
cost was $3.50. How the bureaucrats in Washington

thought you could live for two dollars a day on the frontier was beyond Torn. Just as the food came, a man joined Torn at the table.

It was Jim Murtaugh.

Murtaugh's face had been patched, and stitches had been taken where he'd split his lip. There were dark bruises on his cheek, and one ear was swollen. "I want to talk," he said.

Torn's neighbors at the long table hurriedly shifted to safer locations.

"Talk away," Torn said expansively. "Help yourself to the grub, if you want. Waiter—bring my friend a beer."

Murtaugh tried to be conciliatory. "Look, Torn, I'm sorry about what happened before. I admit, I was out of line with that Winslow woman."

Torn sawed at his beefsteak. If the meat had ever contained a drop of juice, it was news to him.

Murtaugh went on, "You can't blame me, though, can you? I mean, you saw her. She ain't half bad. And you know her reputation. She'll shack up with anything on two legs—and maybe some things on four. So, I asked if I could buy her a drink, and . . . well, I just got a little frustrated, that's all."

Torn looked up. "You thought she'd sold herself to you for the price of a drink?"

Murtaugh slurped some of the beer. "Something like that, I guess. I said I was out of line."

Torn cut his potato. It was raw in the center. "What do you want from me?" he asked.

Murtaugh leaned in closer, so that no one could hear them. Everyone in the restaurant was looking at them, while pretending not to be. Murtaugh said,

"I'll lay my cards on the table, Judge. I'm a developer. If these reservation lands open up, I want to build on them. A lot of people don't like me for that, but it's my job. If I wasn't here, somebody else would be. I ain't just talking for myself, though. There's lots of men here who want to prospect the Red Hills. There's others who want to run cattle in the reservation bottomlands. If we don't chase the Indians off the reservation right now, winter's going to be on us, and it'll be next spring before the land can be put to use. There's a thousand men in Pine City. Delay your ruling, and you'll be condemning those men to a winter in tents, without money and with uncertain supplies. You'll almost certainly be condemning some of them to death. There's children out there, too, little babies. How many of them will die this winter, if their fathers can't go into the Red Hills and bring out lumber for firewood?"

Torn forked a mouthful of onions; they were underdone. He poured salt over everything and tried again.

Murtaugh went on. "What I'm trying to say is that, if we have to wait, a lot of folks are going to lose out, and, well . . . time *is* money, you know." He smiled knowingly at Torn and winked.

Torn washed down his food with the beer. The beer was sour. He put down the mug and smiled. "Why, Mr. Murtaugh, that sounds like a bribe."

"Call it what you want," Murtaugh said. "I'd like to think of it as an invitation to reason. Those Indians have broken their treaty. We both know that. Play around with them in the courts, and me and the rest of these men are going to lose six months' work.

These are hard times back East, Judge. It don't look good to be turning men away from honest labor."

"You finished?" Torn asked.

Murtaugh shrugged. "I guess."

Torn stared hard into Murtaugh's eyes. "Then you listen to me. I won't be bribed, and I won't be persuaded by moral arguments about why we white men need that land. I'll weigh the evidence against the Indians. I'll do what *I* feel is right—no one else. I hope I make that clear, because I'm getting tired of repeating it."

Murtaugh tapped his fingertips on the table. When he spoke, his voice was soft, deadly soft. "All right, Judge. I've tried to reason with you. Now we'll do it the other way." He rose. "You got nobody to blame for what happens but yourself."

Torn had gone back to his leathery steak. He looked up, smiling again. "Now, *that* sounds like a threat."

Murtaugh's eyes were bullets. "Like I said, Judge. Call it what you want." He turned and shoved his way out of the restaurant.

CHAPTER

6

COUNCIL BUTTE WAS THREE MILES NORTHWEST
of Pine City, along Rosewood Creek. The butte was
an outlier of the Red Hills, a plug of reddish sand-
stone, worn down by eons of wind and weather; it
could be seen for miles over the prairie. The Indians
had used it for a landmark and council grounds from
the time they had first ventured onto the plains.

Torn sat on a camp chair, across the creek from
the butte, facing north, the direction from which the
Indians would come. Congressman Van Horne sat
to Torn's right. Van Horne had abandoned the ridic-
ulous buckskin outfit for a formal gray suit and top
hat. The Indian Agent, Larrabee, stood behind them.
He looked like he'd already been drinking. There
was another chair for Major Darcy, which he would

occupy after the tribe's arrival. Red blankets were
spread on the ground for the Indians to sit on. The
four men from the Indian Agency had ridden in yesterday afternoon. They had been greeted as heroes,
lauded for their show of bravery in the face of over-
whelming odds.

Most of Pine City's population was here, men and
women. A few of the men had legal cases against
the Indians. Most were just curious. Many were
armed, and Torn worried that there'd be trouble.
Torn saw Murtaugh, with Pete Gallagher nearby.
Well, that was no surprise. Off to one side was the
press, its distinguished members pushing and shoving for the best vantage points. Penelope Winslow
was there, pushing and shoving with the best of
them. She saw Torn and looked away, still angry
with him. Photographers primed their plates, waiting
for the grand procession of the Northern Cheyenne
into the council area, ready to record the historic
occasion.

With a blare of trumpets, the four troops of cavalry
rode in from Fort Connor, led by Major Darcy. The
trumpets played "Garryowen," the Seventh Cavalry's war song, and the crowd applauded. "There's
the boy's that'll see to them Injuns," someone
shouted.

"Yeah—if we don't do it first," said somebody
else, and a lot of people laughed.

The soldiers were armed with carbines and sa-
bers. They wore black felt helmets with yellow
horsehair plumes. Gold braid was looped over the
chests of their tight blue jackets, and their boots and
belts were polished till they gleamed. "They look

good in those new uniforms, don't they?" said Van Horne in his usual pompous tone.

Torn was less enthusiastic. "They look too much like Prussians for my taste," he said.

"That's the idea behind the uniform change," the congressman explained, looking down his beak-like nose. "Instill in them the will to win, like the Prussians. I'll bet your rebels never had uniforms like that."

Torn had to laugh. "Most of the men in my old regiment were lucky to have shoes, much less uniforms."

The soldiers paraded once around the council ground. They formed up on Clay's right—three troops in line, facing the council area, with the fourth troop in reserve. It was a formation that could become a battle order very quickly.

"We're lucky to have Darcy and his men here," Van Horne said. "The rest of the regiment is with General Custer down South, chasing Ku Kluxers and moonshiners."

The officers' wives stood in a tight group near their men. Torn could tell Darcy's wife because of the way the rest of them catered to her. The yellow silk dress she was wearing must have cost her husband a year's pay.

Noon came. The cavalry held their horses motionless in the broiling sun. Now and then one of the horses tossed its head or snuffled. Torn could imagine the men cursing as their fancy uniforms became ruined with sweat.

All eyes searched the horizon for dust, for a sign

that the Cheyenne were coming. But there was nothing.

An hour passed. The troops were allowed to dismount and rest. Torn checked his watch.

Reluctantly, Torn stood. He turned to the crowd. "All right, ladies and gentlemen. It's past time. Let's begin."

Torn turned his camp chair around. A portable table had been set up there, with paper for taking notes. Torn sat at the table. He folded his hands and said, "I'm here to conduct an inquiry into alleged violations by the Cheyenne Indians of their treaty with the United States." He turned to Van Horne, "I believe your staff has gathered witnesses for me, Congressman?"

"That's right, Judge," said Van Horne. At least ten of Van Horne's people were staying in Pine City.

"Call the first one," Torn said.

Van Horne nodded to one of his eager young aides. The aide led a man forward, a cattleman from the look of his hide vest and wide-brimmed hat. Torn poised his pencil, "Your name?"

"Highland Hixson, your honor. I own a ranch over on Strawberry Flats. That's about twenty-five miles west of here. I had some cattle stole back in September. The seventeenth, it was."

"How many head?"

"Near thirty—twenty-eight to be exact. The, uh, value on that is six hundred and nineteen dollars. I already put a claim against the tribe."

"You think Indians stole them?"

"I don't think it was Injuns—I *know* it was. Here's an arrow I found in one of my animals."

He handed the arrow to Torn, who showed it to Larrabee. "It's Cheyenne, all right," said the Indian Agent. "See those wavy lines down the stem? That's the mark of the Kit Fox Soldiers, Standing Deer's war band."

Hixson went on, "I seen 'em, too, Judge. About two dozen there was, feathered to beat the band. And when me and the boys followed them, we found our stock butchered—cut up alive without a piece of meat taken. It's only Injuns that does that."

Torn said, "Would you recognize any of the Indians if you saw them again?"

"Naw, your honor. They was too far away. Anyways, all Injuns look alike to me."

That remark brought a laugh from the crowd. When the laughter died, Torn said, "Thank you, Mr. Hixson. You are dismissed, subject to recall."

"Say, Judge," said Hixson, scuffing a boot toe in the dust. "When will I be getting that six hundred and nineteen dollars?"

"You'll be notified," Torn said. "The claim has to go through Washington, so I wouldn't expect it in a hurry. Next case."

There was a parade of witnesses. Torn stopped counting at ten. They all told pretty much the same story. Sometimes it was cattle that had been stolen, sometimes horses. Always the tracks led to the Red Hills reservation. Frequently the thieves were seen, but at a distance. There were always about two dozen, with feathers. Like the bunch that had jumped Torn.

When the witnesses were done, Torn sat back and rubbed his eyes.

"I'd say that evidence was pretty conclusive," Van Horne said.

Torn didn't know. He looked at his notes. "I was at Standing Deer's camp in the Red Hills yesterday. I didn't see any horses there that would match these descriptions of stolen animals. I didn't see many horses of any kind."

Larrabee said, "Judge—there's a hundred places in those hills they could be hiding stolen stock."

Torn said, "Has anyone been physically injured— or even attacked—by these Indians?"

"No," Larrabee said. "But it's only a matter of . . ."

"Two riders!" somebody shouted. It was one of the cavalry pickets. "Coming from the north! They're Indians!"

The crowd was galvanized. Darcy ordered his soldiers to mount. Torn rose and trained his eyes past the butte. He saw the dust now. The riders were coming hard. They were bare chested. Sunlight gleamed off something on one's chest.

"It's Standing Deer," Torn said.

The crowd buzzed. They pressed forward. Some of the cavalry horses whinnied nervously.

With Standing Deer was his son, Runs With the Wind. When they were within fifty yards of Torn, the two Indians halted their horses, seemingly in midstride. Standing Deer slid from his wicker saddle, tossing the bridle rope to his son. While Runs With the Wind held the horses, Standing Deer came forward.

The council area had grown quiet. Even Penelope Winslow seemed taken in by the moment.

Standing Deer was not wearing the ceremonial

dress of council. Neither was he painted for war. He stopped in front of the red blanket. He looked directly at Torn. "I am called Standing Deer. I am war leader of the Kit Fox Soldiers."

Torn stood stiffly. His voice was formal. "You are welcome, Standing Deer." He indicated the blanket, "Would you . . . ?"

"I have not come to smoke the council pipe with you, Claytorn." The old chief pronounced Torn's name as if it were one word. "I have come because I believe you are an honest man, and I want you to know how it is with us."

Standing Deer stood tall. His guttural words had dignity. "My father, Red Hawk, was the last free chief of our tribe. He was the last chief to die without knowing the white man. I would have wished for the same fate, but my destiny has been otherwise. I never wanted the treaty with your people, Claytorn. I would have fought forever. I made the peace for my son, Runs With the Wind, and my daughter, Tall Woman. So that they, and their children, might live.

"I asked nothing of the white man but what was promised to my people by the treaty. But those promises were lies. We did not like the model farm, but we were willing to learn its use." Standing Deer pointed at Larrabee, "But this man would not teach us how to grow the corn. This man cheated us out of our beef ration."

"That's a lie!" Larrabee said.

Standing Deer went on, "My people starve to death, and they are not fed. They catch the white man's diseases, but this man will not send white doctors to care for them."

Larrabee swore, "Oh, for . . . !"

"We are accused of leaving the reservation to hunt buffalo. This is true. I myself have led the hunting parties."

There was a buzz from the crowd.

Standing Deer continued. "We are also accused of stealing the white man's horses and cattle. This is not true. We are accused of seeking war. This is not true, either. The truth is that this man, and others, are trying to force us into war."

Larrabee's face was flushed, either from anger or drink. He said, "That's the most . . ."

"These men want a reason to steal our land," Standing Deer said. "They already plan to send my people south, to the reservations around Fort Sill."

Congressman Van Horne spoke up, blustering, "I assure you, Chief, there's been no final . . ."

"I have seen that land!" Standing Deer said, and his voice quavered. "The shaking sickness is there. My people will die from it."

The chief appealed to Torn. "What would you do, Claytorn? Would you give up your land, or would you fight for it? Would you go meekly to the white man's death camps? Would you die like a dog, or like a man?"

Torn said nothing. There was nothing he could say.

"At least this way, we will retain our honor," Standing Deer said. "When they speak of us in future days, they will say we died well."

Torn said, "Standing Deer, I told you before that I am here to help. You have said many things today. I must learn the truth of them. This takes time."

"No," said the chief. "There is no more time." He wrenched the heavy gold medal from his neck, and he threw it on the blanket at Torn's feet. "When next you see me, I shall be painted for war."

"Wait!" Torn said.

He moved closer to Standing Deer, so that no one else could hear. "Why did you save me from those men, the other day?"

The Indian replied proudly. "I would not have my enemies say that it was I who killed you."

"Do you know who those men were? And who were 'the others' that your son said stayed illegally on the reservation?"

"You must learn these things for yourself. Otherwise, you will not believe."

"But how can I learn, if you will not give me time?"

Standing Deer considered. Then he said, "Two suns, Claytorn. I will give you two suns. Then there will be war."

Standing Deer turned and started back for his horse.

In the crowd, Torn saw movement. Someone stepped forward with a raised pistol. It was Pete Gallagher.

With his left hand, Torn knocked Gallagher's gun aside. With his right, he threw a punch that caught Gallagher flush on the jaw. Gallagher staggered sideways, lost his balance and fell on the seat of his pants. Torn drew his .45 and turned on the crowd.

"Anybody that moves is a dead man," he said.

The crowd murmured, but no one moved.

If Standing Deer heard the commotion, he gave no evidence. He did not look back. He took his bridle rope from Runs With the Wind, and he vaulted onto his horse. The two Indians galloped off.

For a moment, there was silence. Then everyone started talking at once. All except Torn. He picked up Standing Deer's medal. On one side of the medal was a likeness of President Grant, and a date, 1872. On the other side, the American eagle and "In God We Trust."

"A souvenir," Van Horne explained. "From the chief's visit to Washington last year."

Torn scraped the metal with his fingernail. "Brass," he said. "It's not even real gold."

"I should hope not," Van Horne said. "You don't think we'd give a savage real gold, do you?"

CHAPTER 7

MAJOR DARCY DETACHED HIMSELF FROM THE formation. Accoutrements jingling, he trotted his sleek black charger over to where Torn stood with Congressman Van Horne.

Van Horne was in high dudgeon. "Did you hear that savage, Darcy? Did you hear the way he spoke to me? Have you ever met anyone so brazen?"

"The Seventh will take the shine off him," Darcy promised, running a finger along his waxed moustache. He was resplendent in helmet, red sash and white gloves, and he knew it. To Torn, he said, "All right, Judge. Let's get on with it. I want to have my men in the field before sundown. If we march all night, we can be in position to attack Standing Deer's camp at dawn. Issue your ruling, or whatever it is

you have to do. It doesn't have to be in writing—
your verbal authority's good enough for me."

Torn had been looking thoughtfully at Standing
Deer's Washington medal, letting it dangle by its
broken chain. Now he snapped up the medal and put
it in his coat pocket. Sweat ran down his back in the
hot sun. He said, "I'm not issuing anything, Major."

There were angry murmurs from the crowd.

Van Horne swore. "You heard the evidence, man.
It's . . ."

"What evidence?" Torn said. "You've got horses
missing that are never found, stolen by Indians that
can't be identified. You couldn't convict a white man
on that kind of evidence, what makes it good enough
to convict Indians?"

Van Horne looked stunned. So did Major Darcy.
The crowd grew louder.

Torn went on, "And what if the Cheyenne are
guilty? It sounds to me like this is the work of a small
band. Do we punish the whole tribe because of a few
habitual criminals? That would be like kicking everyone out of Pine City because a few men there are
pickpockets."

"There's a difference," said Major Darcy smugly.
"The men in Pine City don't scalp and torture. I
suppose you've never seen what the Cheyenne do
to their . . ."

"Yes, I have seen it," Torn said. "I've also seen
the inside of a Yankee prison camp, and it's a toss-
up which was worse."

Darcy reddened under his crested helmet. The
crowd was in an uproar. Congressman Van Horne
had to shout to make himself heard. "The Indians

No one told him. "Find him yourself!" somebody shouted.

Larrabee must have slipped away. He must be part of the crowd that had already started back for town. He probably couldn't wait any longer for another drink.

"Thanks," Torn told the crowd.

Torn took up the reins of his rented roan, and he mounted. As he did, Major Darcy sidled his charger close. He said, "I'm not done with you, Sesesh."

Torn stopped. "Don't push it, Major."

Torn wheeled his horse and started for Pine City. Behind him, he heard bugles, as the cavalry returned to Fort Connor. Torn joined the procession of men on horseback and foot, heading toward town. He spurred his horse ahead, to get away from the choking dust. He ignored the taunts and jeers of the men around him. "Indian lover! Get out now, while you still can!"

After some searching, Torn found Larrabee in the Red Elephant Saloon. The tarpaper shack was squalid even for Pine City. Inside, it was nearly empty. It stank of stale beer and tobacco. Larrabee stood at the crude bar, pouring whiskey into a tin cup; he tossed the drink down.

Torn joined Larrabee at the bar. As Larrabee went to pour more whiskey, Torn took the bottle out of his hand.

Larrabee started. He reached for the bottle, but Clay held it away. "Left the council a bit early, didn't you?" Torn said.

Larrabee recovered, "Maybe I got tired of hearing my name run down."

"Let's you and me talk," Torn said.

The Indian agent looked wary. "What about?"

"Standing Deer. He says you're trying to starve the Cheyenne into starting a war."

Larrabee eyed the bottle thirstily. "That's nonsense. Why would I do that?"

"You tell me. He says you never issued their beef rations."

Larrabee licked his lips. "That's a lie, too. Every bit of food promised by that treaty was delivered, and on time. I've got the weigh slips and issue tickets to prove it, if you want to see them."

"I do want to see them," Torn said. "What about doctors? Standing Deer says you wouldn't give his people access to them."

"You know Indians, Judge. They won't accept white doctors. They want to do things their own way, even if it means killing half the tribe. I tried to get doctors to them last winter—I did—but the Cheyenne wouldn't let them into their camps."

Larrabee grabbed for the bottle. Torn pulled it back. "Then why would Standing Deer say what he did?"

"How do I know?" Larrabee said. "So he could fool you into thinking he's been mistreated, I guess. Standing Deer wants to have it both ways. He wants to be able to break his part of the treaty, but he wants us to live up to ours."

"I thought you liked Indians," Torn said.

"I do. I do like Indians."

"You have an Indian wife, don't you? Cheyenne?"

"Yes, but that doesn't change what's happening. Do you think I like watching those people lose their land? I don't. But I can't lie and say they haven't been breaking the treaty."

Torn slid the bottle forward on the bar. He poured Larrabee a drink. Relief flooded the Indian agent's bearded face.

Torn said, "Tell me about yourself, Mr. Larrabee. Have you been in these parts long?"

Larrabee took the tin cup and drank. He let out a sigh of satisfaction. "I been here since the '50's. I done a little bit of everything in my time—drove a stagecoach, bossed a freight train, run a relay station."

"How'd you become Indian agent?"

Larrabee's cup was empty again. He looked hopefully for more, and Torn obliged. Larrabee said, "I traded with the Cheyenne for years. When the reservation was established, it was natural that I became the licensed trader. Then the agent's job opened up." He shrugged, "I wasn't really expecting it. I guess they needed somebody who knew the Cheyenne."

Torn tilted the bottle over the cup. Then he stopped. "What do you know about the Prometheus Company?"

A worried look crossed Larrabee's face. "N-nothing," he said, trying overly hard to be casual. "What's the Prometheus Company?"

Torn continued to hold the bottle suspended. "I don't know, but half the men in Pine City work for it. Who runs it?"

"I told you, Judge, I don't know. Why are you picking on me, anyway? I ain't done nothing. I just do what I'm told."

Torn raised an eyebrow. "Told by who?"

Larrabee was really worried now. He was falling apart. "It's just a figure of speech, Judge. A joke, all right? Leave me alone, will you? I've got a wife and kids. I can't afford to lose..."

Larrabee stopped. He looked over his shoulder, and there was fear on his face. Torn turned. Pete Gallagher was standing in the saloon door, listening.

Gallagher sauntered in, followed by half-a-dozen shoulder-hitters. Through the saloon door, Torn could see a crowd outside. One corner of Gallagher's mouth turned up in anticipation. There was no mistaking his intentions.

Torn wore his six-gun under his coat. He went for it. Larrabee reached around and knocked the pistol from Torn's hand. Torn heard Gallagher shout, "Get him!"

Gallagher was the first one in. Torn hit the big man square on the cheek, and he went down. Torn turned, grabbed Larrabee's arm and swung him into the toughs. That tangled them up for a second. Torn started over the bar, intending to get the shotgun. Too late, he saw the bartender waiting for him with a sap. He saw the weighted end coming toward him. It grew big in his eyes. There was an explosion. Then blackness.

TORN CAME TO.

His head hurt. He was sitting up, in a chair, with his hands tied behind him. Outside, the sun was setting. There was a crowd out there, yelling for blood. His blood.

Inside the saloon, Pete Gallagher and a half-dozen toughs were passing a bottle. On the bar before them lay a coiled rope. One end had been tied into a hangman's noose.

Gallagher saw that Torn was awake. He rubbed the bruise that Torn had planted on his cheek. "Well, well. Here's the star of the show. It's you they're calling for out there, Judge. How does that make you feel?"

"Go to hell," Torn said.

Gallagher said, "You know, Judge, you got a big mouth."

Torn said, "You know, Gallagher, you've got a little brain."

Gallagher crossed the room, fist cocked. He measured Torn for a punch, and Torn realized that Gallagher was looking to take out his eye. Gallagher swung. Torn turned his head. Gallagher's fist tore open Torn's eyebrow. Blood spurted; Torn could feel it running down his face. Another blow. Again Torn ducked. Again the blow ripped into his brow. A third blow to the pit of his stomach doubled him over in the chair, retching.

"That's enough," said a voice. "Don't kill him." The voice was Jim Murtaugh's.

Torn looked up. It was hard to see because of all the blood.

Murtaugh stood with his hands in his pockets, grinning at Torn. "Hello, Judge. As you may have guessed, your term of office is about to expire. You been tried and found guilty—Judge Lynch, presiding."

"Guilty of what?" Torn said.

"I hadn't thought about that," Murtaugh said. He shrugged. "Being an Indian lover will do for a start."

Torn had a hard time hearing. His face was puffy. There was blood all over him, and his skull felt like it was broken where he'd been hit with the sap. Gallagher and his men were passing the whiskey again.

Torn sneered at them. "What's the matter, Gallagher? You have to work up the guts to do it?"

Gallagher laughed pleasantly. He wiped whiskey

out of his short beard. "No, Judge. That ain't it at all. We're just waiting for dark. See, after we hang you, we're going to make a bonfire out of you. Kind of like Halloween come a week early."

Torn said, "You won't pull this off, Murtaugh."

Murtaugh looked unimpressed. "Anything can happen on the frontier, Judge. You should know that. You hear that crowd. The official story will be that a mob broke into this saloon and took you out. You were then hanged 'by person or persons unknown.' Tomorrow, everybody will feel real sorry about what happened, but . . . what the hell, what's done is done, and meanwhile there's an Indian war to be fought. Before long, you'll be forgotten. You'll be an unfortunate footnote to history."

Torn had a tough time talking with all the blood in his mouth. "You're a pig, Murtaugh."

Murtaugh slapped Torn hard, making his head snap back in the chair.

"The hell with waiting," Murtaugh snarled. "Finish those drinks, and let's get this over with."

The men downed their cups or took a last quick gulp from Gallagher's bottle. A commotion could be heard outside. It sounded like a fight.

"You got the torches?" Murtaugh asked Gallagher.

The big man nodded. "They're right outside the . . ."

At nearby Fort Connor, the trumpets began sounding Assembly.

"What the . . .?" Murtaugh said.

The commotion outside grew louder. A man stuck his head in the door, breathless. "Army patrol just rode in, Jim. The Indian Agency's on fire. Major

Darcy's called out the battalion."

At the fort, they were already sounding Stable Call.

"You still want to hang the judge?" Gallagher asked his boss.

Murtaugh looked out the door. A lot of the crowd was already leaving, going for weapons and horses. A lynching appealed to them, but it was not nearly as exciting as the prospect of attacking an Indian village.

Murtaugh did not want to lose control of the situation. He went out the door of the house and raised his voice to the crowd. "Come on, boys! We can't let the army beat us to that Indian camp! I want the Pine City Volunteers in the saddle in fifteen minutes!"

There was a shout, and the rest of the crowd broke up, running. Murtaugh said, "Get 'em ready, Pete." He turned to a couple of Gallagher's toughs. "Brandnauer, Gerson—you two stay here. Watch the judge. When we're out of town, kill him. Dump the body. We can always say the Indians got him."

"Right," Brandnauer said. Gerson nodded. Brandnauer was big and blond, with thick lips. Gerson was a pinch-faced, nasty-looking little man.

At the fort, the bugles were sounding Boots and Saddles now.

Murtaugh started out the saloon door after his men. He stopped and looked back, grinning. "Have fun, Judge."

Brandnauer and Gerson both carried revolvers. The big man had a Sharps rifle as well. They went to the door, watching the activity outside.

Torn was in a fog of pain. Things drifted in and out. He heard a distant, rhythmic rumble. That must be the cavalry riding out of Fort Connor. They were followed by the Pine City Volunteers, whooping and hollering, half of them drunk, not riding in any kind of formation.

When the last riders were gone, an eerie quiet descended on Pine City. Torn's guards turned from the door. "I don't see why I had to stay," complained Gerson, the nasty-looking one. "I had to stay last time."

Brandnauer, the big blond, was looking around the saloon. He said, "Hey, this ain't so bad. Aside from killing him, we got nothing to do while they're gone, and there's all this liquor to drink. You could get yourself shot in an Injun fight."

"Yeah," Gerson whined. "But we won't get no loot. We won't get no women."

Brandnauer examined the bottles of liquor, scratching his head. "I was at Sand Creek with Chivington, and there wasn't no loot to speak of. Just moccasins and beads and junk like that—nothing worth money. And the women! Man, they smell bad and they got fleas, and if you turn your back on them they'll slit your throat."

"No different than the girls in the Club Room," Gerson retorted. "And you got to pay for them."

Gerson wandered over to the prisoner. He spit on Torn's face. Then he laughed. It was a grating, cackling laugh.

"When do you figure they'll be back?" Brandnauer said.

"Tomorrow afternoon's my guess," Gerson said.

"With Standing Deer's scalp on a pole. Bet the boss throws one of his big parties tomorrow night."

Brandnauer chose a bottle. He couldn't read the labels, and that hadn't made his decision easier. "I'm having my party right now," he said. "What about you, Joey? Pick your poison."

Gerson pointed. "That one there, with the bird on the label."

Brandnauer uncorked the bottle and passed it to Gerson. "How 'bout you, Judge? Want a drink?"

Torn said nothing.

"Sure," said Brandnauer, "you must want a drink." He chuckled and picked up a brass spittoon. The spitoon was filled with spit and cigar butts and dirt. Brandnauer took a jug of water from behind the bar and poured some into the spittoon. He shook the mixture up. Gerson watched, cackling with anticipation.

Brandnauer held the spittoon under Torn's nose. "Here you go."

Torn turned his head. The smell was enough to make him sick. Gerson laughed.

Brandnauer pressed the spittoon closer. "Go on, Judge. Drink it."

Brandnauer forced the spittoon against Torn's clamped teeth. The rank liquid splashed down Torn's chin, mixing with the blood on his shirt. Gerson was howling with laughter now. Brandnauer stamped on Torn's toes. Torn screamed, and Brandnauer went to dump the liquid in his open mouth.

There was a pounding on the door.

A woman's voice shouted, "Hey! Is anybody in there?"

Brandnauer dropped the spittoon and picked up his rifle. Gerson drew his revolver. "Who's there?" he shouted.

The woman's voice was brassy, her accent Irish. "The name's Molly Malloy, if it's any of your business. I just rode into this miserable dump of a town, and I need a place to spend the night. Where the hell is everybody?"

Gerson and Brandnauer looked at each other. "Are you alone?" Gerson asked the girl through the door.

"So far I am," she said impatiently.

"Are you a whore?" Brandnauer asked.

"No, I'm the Virgin resting on the Flight into Egypt. Now, are you going to let me in, or do I find somewhere else to spend the night?"

"No," Gerson said. "Don't do that."

"Wait," said Brandnauer, hurriedly unbarring the door. "Come in."

Brandnauer threw open the door. Penny Winslow stood there, pointing a Bulldog pistol at the two men.

Penny spoke in her normal voice now. "All right. Both of you move back."

The two men looked at her in surprise.

"Get back, I said." Penny flourished the pistol at them.

The two men backed up. Penny followed them into the room, pistol leveled. Then she saw Torn, and she winced at his battered face. That's when they went for her.

Gerson leaped. Penny fired from reflex. Gerson crashed into her and fell to the ground. Penny recovered her balance and swung the pistol at Brandnauer, but he got there first, grabbing her gun arm.

He dragged her toward him, pulling at the pistol with his free hand. She tried to get away. They struggled. There was a shot. Brandnauer stepped back. He sat heavily, holding his stomach. Then he slumped over, moaning.

Penny held the smoking pistol. Her hand was shaking.

"Thanks," Torn told her. "I'm surprised you came. Aren't you missing your big story?"

"Yeah. Well, maybe I have a bigger story here."

Gerson was dead, Brandnauer was dying. Penny searched their belts for a knife. Torn said, "Where'd you get that British pistol?"

"In London. It was a gift from General Gordon— Chinese Gordon. I had . . ."

"I know. You went to him for an interview. You ever shoot a man before?"

"You'd be surprised what I've had to do," she said.

She found a knife in Gerson's belt. She knelt by Torn's chair, poising the blade over the his bonds. "Now, about that interview," she said.

Torn shook his head. "No interview."

Penny hesitated, then she sighed. "Oh, well. I tried." She began cutting the rope. "You're pigheaded, you know that?"

"Stop talking so much, and cut me loose."

She was through the rope. While Torn rubbed feeling into his wrists and hands, Penny cut a piece of her dress and wrapped his forehead with it to stop the bleeding.

"You look worse every time I see you," she said. "Do people always use you for a punching bag?"

"No," said Torn. "Sometimes they shoot at me, too."

She wrinkled her nose. "You smell like old cigars."

"In the tobacco business, they call it aging."

Torn stood. He staggered toward the door. The blood drained from his head, and he almost passed out. Waves of pain broke over him.

Penny grabbed him. She got him moving forward. The feel of his legs working again brought him back to life. A few steps, and they were outside. The crisp night air cleared Torn's head a bit.

"At least when it's cold like this, you can't smell the garbage in the streets," Penny said.

Torn's feet found their rhythm. "I'm going to the reservation," he said. "I've got to get there before dawn. That's when Darcy and Murtaugh will attack. It'll be a massacre, Sand Creek all over again."

"I'm going, too," Penny said, hurrying to keep up with him.

"I hope you can ride, then. Because I'm not going to wait for you."

"Ride?" Penny laughed, "Listen, you'd . . ."

"I know, I know. I'd be surprised what you can do."

Penny said, "Where are we going to get horses, anyway?"

"We're going to steal them, what do you think?"

CHAPTER 9

TORN AND PENNY RODE HARD FOR THE RES-
ervation. The air had turned raw and cold. A bank
of clouds had moved in, obscuring the stars. They
followed the trail left by the soldiers and Pine City
Volunteers. The trail didn't head for the Agency,
where the fire was. It led straight for Standing Deer's
camp in the Red Hills. Darcy and Murtaugh were
out for blood.

After an hour, Torn and Penny stopped to rest
the horses.

The wind had picked up. Torn turned his back to
it. His head was killing him. Blood had seeped
through the improvised bandage, and now it was
freezing to his skin. His old war wound was stiff from
the damp and cold. "Going to be a storm," he said.

Penny flapped her arms, trying to warm herself. She hadn't brought a coat. "Here," said Torn, and he handed her what was left of his black suit coat.

"Won't you get cold?" she said.

Torn laughed. "I'm supposed to be tough."

Penny donned the coat gratefully. "It looks like your friend Standing Deer has gone back on his word to you."

"That's what it *looks* like," Torn said.

"What do you mean? If Standing Deer didn't burn the Agency, who did?"

"I don't know. I don't know what to believe, any more. I do know that if it's the same two dozen men that have caused all the other trouble around here, they probably won't be in that village right now. Which means the army will kill every Indian but the ones they want. Darcy and Murtaugh will stage a massacre and call it a victory for civilization."

Penny turned up the collar of Torn's coat. "Not many men would have risked their lives the way you did today, not for a tribe of Indians. That took courage."

Torn shrugged. He felt uncomfortable talking about such things. "Yeah. I haven't had a good day unless somebody puts a rope around my neck."

"Why don't you just sit in a courtroom like a regular judge?"

Torn rubbed his frozen hands together. He blew on them. "Sometimes you have to go outside the courtroom to get justice."

She looked at him skeptically. "You sound like a knight errant."

"Let's say I've been the victim of an injustice. I

can't repair the damage that's been done to me, but I can try to help other people." He gathered his horse's reins. "Now, we've had enough talk. These animals are rested. Let's get going."

As they entered the Red Hills, the temperature continued to fall. The sky was heavy with moisture; it had turned creamy white and it seemed to glow, casting an unworldly illumination over the nighttime landscape.

Torn and Penny turned down the narrow valley. They ran into stragglers from the Volunteers, pushing forward through wind and cold. Most had left town in a hurry, and they weren't dressed for the deteriorating weather. Other stragglers sat, exhausted or drunk, beside the trail. Torn wondered how many would freeze to death before the night was out.

The Volunteers nudged one another as Clay and Penny rode by. "Lookit who it is. Lookit what they done to him."

"I thought he was dead."

"He would have been, if we hadn't . . ."

The voices faded. The stragglers dropped behind. Further on, Torn and Penny encountered the main column of Volunteers, with the soldiers ahead of them. The column was dismounted. Men were stamping their feet in the cold. At the head of the column, the officers and civilian leaders were holding a council of war.

The members of the council stood with their collars turned up against the wind. Some, like Darcy, were like little boys, almost giggling in anticipation of what was to come. Others, like Captain Harman, looked more sober-minded. Murtaugh and Pete Gallagher were there. So was Larrabee, pulling his beard. Off to one side were the gentlemen of the press. Mentally, they had already written their stories about the destruction of the Indian village— gallant victory or brutal massacre, depending upon what slant their papers wanted. All they needed now was the casualty count.

The sergeant of the guard passed Torn and Penny through to the council. Murtaugh saw Torn and he started. Pete Gallagher's jaw dropped. Involuntarily, Murtaugh took a step back and started for his six-gun. Then he remembered all the witnesses, and he let his gun hand drop.

Torn smiled. "Evening, Murtaugh."

Murtaugh recovered quickly. "Evening, Judge." He nodded to Penny, "Miss Winslow."

Torn said, "Maybe some time we can finish that talk we were having."

Murtaugh smiled, too. "We will, we will. I'm sure of it."

"Gallagher, you might like to join us," Torn said.

The big man grinned, "Wouldn't miss it for the world, Judge."

Congressman Van Horne looked puzzled. "You told us Torn was dead, Murtaugh." Van Horne was dressed like Buffalo Bill again, all fringed buckskins and weapons.

Murtaugh shrugged. "Somebody must have got the story wrong. I just told you what I heard."

Major Darcy seemed amused by Torn's bruised and battered condition. "Well, well, what happened to you, Sesesh?"

"I walked into a wall," Torn told him.

Van Horne said, "You've come for nothing, you know. Standing Deer has attacked the property of the United States government, and he's about to pay for it."

Major Darcy added, "After tonight, the citizens of Dakota will never have to worry about the Cheyenne again."

Torn said. "Do you know it was Indians that burned the Agency? Did anyone see them? Larrabee, were you there?"

Larrabee wouldn't meet Torn's gaze. "No. The Agency was on fire when I got back."

"Oh, come on," Van Horne told Torn, "who else could it have been?"

Major Darcy said, "It's too late to argue now. The attack is ready to go in." He looked at his watch. "It's time, gentlemen. You know your dispositions. Are there any questions before we move out?"

There weren't, and Darcy turned to Penny, "Miss Winslow, you will remain in the rear with the other members of the press."

"Oh, no, I won't," she said. "I'm . . ."

"I will not dispute the matter with you, Miss Winslow. If you won't remain here voluntarily, I'll have you placed under arrest."

Penny boiled with silent fury. Torn grinned at her fate. He didn't want her along, either. Darcy added, "The same goes for you, Judge."

"No it doesn't," Torn told him. "I'm going with the attack. I'm a senior public official, and I have that right. I intend to keep an eye on Mr. Murtaugh, here, and his 'Volunteers.' I want to be sure there's no Indian babies bashed to death, no women raped and mutilated."

"This is a military mission." Darcy said. "You hold no commission."

"I was a colonel of infantry, in the war. This isn't the first dawn attack I've seen."

Darcy sneered, "You weren't with a real army in the war."

"We whipped you enough."

Beneath his waxed moustache, Darcy's lips tightened with anger. He started to reply, but Murtaugh spoke first, "Let him come." Then he added, "Maybe the Indians will put a bullet in him."

Torn said, "You mean, if you don't beat them to it?"

Murtaugh smiled.

Darcy said, "Very well, then. You may come. Just keep out of my way." He spoke louder, "Gentlemen, rejoin your troops. Prepare to move out."

Torn and Penny started from the council. Around them, men were getting ready for battle. Torn heard metallic clicks. He heard the shuffling of hoofs, the low whisper of conversation. The smell of gun oil was strong in the cold air. The first flakes of snow started to fall.

They reached the horses. Torn checked his weapons. He had taken Brandnauer's pistol, an old Army .44. He had no idea where his own pistol had gone. Brandnauer had only carried five reloads in his pockets. Torn had retrieved his Spencer carbine and saber-knife from the stable, where he'd left them. He thought about borrowing Penny's Bulldog pistol for the attack, but he knew that she should have something to defend herself with.

He was ready to go. He turned to Penny. "Be seeing you."

"Yeah," said Penny. Torn's black coat was oversized on her, and she snuggled in it. Snow lay white on her shoulders.

Torn mounted.

"Judge?" Penny said.

Torn looked down.

"Watch out for yourself," Penny said. Self-consciously, she added, "You know, I didn't go to all the trouble of rescuing you, just to have you do something stupid like get shot in the back. You're a big story to me."

Torn grinned. "I'll do my best to make sure it has a happy ending."

Torn wheeled his horse and rode for the head of the column. The plan was for the troops and Volunteers to enter the broad prairie, form up and charge the Indian camp at first light.

Suddenly, Larrabee stepped out of the snow to Torn's right.

"Judge, I have to talk to you," Larrabee said, slurring his words. "There's some things you have to know."

Torn's horse reared. "There's no time now. I'm worried what Murtaugh and his men will do when they get in that village," said Torn.

"So am I," Larrabee said. He looked over his shoulder, as though he was afraid of being watched.

Torn said, "I'll meet you at the Agency, after the fight."

"All right. But be quick."

Torn rode on. It was snowing heavily now. He reached the head of the column. Darcy was there. So were Captain Harman and Murtaugh, and some officers Torn didn't know. Murtaugh wore a buffalo robe coat. He carried a sawed-off shotgun across his saddle.

Darcy looked down the column and gave the signal to mount. There was the creak of leather as the men swung onto their horses. Darcy waved them forward.

Captain Harman and two Pawnee scouts led the way. Each man in the column concentrated on the back of the man before him. It was just about all that anyone could see in the thick snow. They passed through the narrow gap in the hills, then were out onto the prairie. The Indian camp was invisible before them. The wind whipped the snow into their eyes. Some of the men had trouble holding in their horses.

Sections of cavalry were sent left and right, to strike the camp's flanks. The rest of the soldiers and the Volunteers formed a battle line.

Murtaugh rode over to join his Volunteers. Torn stayed with the soldiers for now. He didn't want to take a bullet in the back during the charge. If Murtaugh wanted to try something afterwards, that was fine with Torn.

Visibility was measured in feet. Major Darcy couldn't see either end of his battle line. When he thought it must be formed up, he motioned it forward.

All around, Torn felt the unseen mass of men heave itself forward, slowly at first, then picking up speed, hoofbeats curiously muffled by the snow. The men had their revolvers out.

They still couldn't see the Indian camp. It was hard to tell how much of the prairie they'd crossed in this snow.

Darcy increased speed. They were at a fast trot now. It was hard to hold the horses in. Darcy turned, "Trumpeter. Sound the Charge."

The trumpeter raised his bugle. The stirring notes of the charge split the snowy silence. A cry went up along the line. Horses bounded forward. Yelling, hollering, troops and Volunteers charged across the prairie. They were riding blind. Torn heard at least one horse go down. He heard the rider's thin scream. He gathered his own reins tight. His pistol was out, but he didn't intend on shooting anyone—except, maybe, Murtaugh.

The cries of the attackers reached a crescendo. There was no firing from the Indian camp. There was no sound at all. That was unusual. Then Torn understood why.

He rode past the remains of lodge fires, black against the snow. Here and there were bits of camp gear, hastily abandoned. Around Torn, the yelling took on a puzzled sound, then faded out. Men rode around the deserted camp in confused circles, as if searching for someone who had vanished into thin air. Which was exactly what Standing Deer had done.

"He's broken out," Torn told Major Darcy. "He's left the reservation, with all his people."

CHAPTER

10

THE LITTLE HEADQUARTERS GROUP RODE
through the deserted Indian camp. Major Darcy was
so mad he could barely hold himself in. Standing Deer
had made a fool of him.

"Sound Recall," he snapped to his trumpeter.

The bugle notes rang out. The snow was still falling, through the wind had died. About the group
there was partially seen movement, as the troops
and Volunteers reformed.

Murtaugh rode up through the snow. "What the
hell happened? When did the Indians get away?"

Darcy's elaborately waxed moustache was rimed
with snow. His voice filled with disgust, as he glanced
at Torn. "No doubt they were breaking camp while
Standing Deer was at the Judge's council, swearing

how he wouldn't go to war for two days. Their tracks are hidden in this snow. There's no way of telling which way they've gone." He swore, "We should have shot Standing Deer when we had the chance."

"I seem to recall someone making the attempt," Murtaugh said bitterly.

"So do I. If he'd succeeded, we'd have been spared all this."

Torn looked around for Pete Gallagher, the man who'd tried to shoot Standing Deer, but he didn't see him.

Van Horne was part of the little group. He looked wet and cold, and he had lost his fancy plainsman's hat. "Which way do you think Standing Deer has gone, Major?"

"West is my guess. To the Yellowstone and Powder River country. It's the only place he'll find free Indians this side of Canada. Any other direction, and he'll run into white settlements."

"Perhaps that's his objective," Van Horne said, "to attack the settlements."

Darcy turned to his adjutant for another opinion. "Captain Harman, you know Standing Deer better than I do. What's your assessment of where he's gone?"

Harman looked uncomfortable, as if that were a question he'd rather not answer. He was duty bound to tell the truth, however. "In my opinion, sir, Standing Deer doesn't have the animals or food for a march to the Yellowstone, not in this weather. For the same reason, I don't think he'll raid the settlements. We'd catch him before he could do much damage. Anyway, he and his people are with their families, and they wouldn't take them on a raid. It's my belief he'll retreat deeper into the Red Hills. It's sacred ground to the Cheyenne. I believe he and his people are determined to make a last stand in there, to sell their lives as dearly as possible."

Darcy considered, then he said, "Send out patrols. An officer and ten men from each troop. They're to concentrate on the western trails and the Red Hills. They'll carry full field gear and rations for three days. They move out in fifteen minutes."

"Yes, sir," Harman said, and he wheeled his horse to carry out the orders.

To Darcy, Van Horne said, "If you're wrong, and the Indians hit the settlements, it will mean the end of all our careers."

"And if I'm right, we'll all be heroes," Darcy said confidently.

Torn said, "What do you intend to do, Major?"

"I intend to catch Standing Deer. I intend to kill him and destroy his people as a fighting force."

"You won't negotiate?"

"Negotiate what? The treaty's broken. The war has begun."

"It's not too late," Torn said. "Nobody's been killed yet—though you've certainly tried hard enough. All we've had so far is a building burned. We can still avoid violence."

"Why should we? We're doing the country a favor by killing off these savages."

"Let me give you one reason," Torn said. "You've got about two dozen reporters attached to this command. Approximately half of them think your soldiers are rapists and baby killers, and if they can get a story that proves them right, they'll plaster it across the country."

Congressman Van Horne cleared his throat. "He's right, Major. We must consider how this will play in the papers. It could hurt a lot of people politically." He was equivocating already, in case something went wrong. "We want to be careful not to make a martyr out of Standing Deer."

"Don't worry," Darcy told him. "The only thing we'll make out of Standing Deer is a corpse." He turned, "Colonel Murtaugh, will your Volunteers remain in the field, sir?"

Murtaugh grinned. "The ones that are needed will. I expect the rest will be heading back to Pine City."

"I'll go with them," Van Horne said. "This is likely to prove a long chase, and I've got a lot of work to catch up on. The Congressional paper flow doesn't stop just because you're in the wilderness, you know. You'll inform me as soon as something happens?"

Darcy nodded, and Van Horne rode off gratefully. All around Torn was the buzz of routine, as men set up camp, picketing their horses and building fires. The snow was letting up. There were six to eight inches on the ground—a warmup for the Dakota winter.

No one seemed to pay much attention to Torn. He gave his horse a light feeding, then started for the Indian Agency, to meet Larrabee. Leaving the prairie, he encountered one of the patrols, starting out. In command was his young acquaintance, Lt. McIntyre.

"Hello, Lieutenant," Torn said.

"Hi, there, Judge," said McIntyre. He peered at

Torn's ripped clothes and bruised face. "What happened to you?"

"Some fellows didn't like my looks, so they tried to change them," Torn said. "They did a pretty fair job, too."

Lt. McIntyre shook his head. "I don't suppose you have any more of those seegars?"

"Nope." Torn grinned. "Fresh out."

"Too bad. That was one of the best smokes I've ever had."

"I'll send you some when I get more," Torn said. "Which way are you headed?"

"West, toward the Badlands."

"Be careful," Clay told him.

Lt. McIntyre grinned boyishly, "I will be, sir. I want to be around to collect those seegars."

McIntyre rejoined his men. Torn urged his already tired horse eastward, toward the Agency. The morning sun struggled to come from behind the clouds. The wind blew warmer. The snow was already starting to melt.

Torn smelled the Agency before he saw it. Even with all the snow that had fallen, the odor of charred wood was strong. Torn came in sight of the Agency, and he reined in. The Agency building itself was gutted, a charred wreck. So was the trading post. The corrals had been broken down. The Agent's house was a little off from the other buildings. It had not been damaged, and there were two horses tied in front.

Torn rode forward. It was quiet. He wondered why the Indians had not burned the Agent's house. Maybe Larrabee's return had frightened them off, or maybe it was the Indians' way of showing displeasure toward the government, but not its representative. Larrabee was married to a Cheyenne woman, after all.

As Torn approached the house, he saw three sets of tracks in the snow. Three people had come to the house. Two were still inside, one with small feet. A bigger man had ridden away. The snow covered the tracks of the Indians who'd burned the Agency.

Torn tied his horse alongside the other two. The front door of the house was closed.

"Larrabee?" he called.

No answer.

Torn opened the door, "Larrabee?"

Still no answer. Torn stepped inside. The two-room house was quiet. Torn thought he smelled gunpowder.

"Larrabee, are you . . . ?"

He stopped. A man was lying on the floor, just outside the bedroom door. It was Larrabee.

Torn drew the .44 he'd taken from Brandnauer. He knelt beside the Indian agent. Larrabee was lying on his face, dead. He'd been that way for about two hours. He'd been shot in the back of the head, at close range. Clay smelled burnt hair and flesh. A congealing pool of blood lay beneath Larrabee's head.

Clay cocked the pistol. The small-footed person was in the other room—dead or alive, Clay didn't know. Clay paused beside the bedroom door. He took a deep breath. He stepped over the body and in the door, sweeping the room with the pistol, ready to fire.

He pulled up in surprise. The room was empty.

CHAPTER 11

TORN TURNED AROUND IN DISBELIEF.

It was impossible. The house couldn't be empty. No one could have left without making tracks in the snow, unless they used magic, or had wings.

Which meant they were still here.

Torn looked around the two rooms. He pulled the woolen blanket-rug from the living room floor. He stamped on the plank floor with his boot heel, until he hit a hollow spot.

He got on his hands and knees. Whoever had made the trap door—Larrabee, presumably—had done a good job. Even close up, the joinings were hard to see. Torn felt around until he found the pull-up, which was under a pine knot.

He lifted the trap door and looked down into a

small, damp hole. A narrow tunnel, shored with timber, led off the hole. It was a bolt hole, built as a last defense against Indian attack. There was a coulee about seventy-five yards from the house, and Torn guessed that the tunnel ended there.

Torn got into the hole. He squatted and peered down the dark tunnel, but saw nothing. The mud was disturbed. Someone—the small-footed person—had crawled through this passageway, and not long before.

Torn climbed out of the hole. There was no point in following the small-footed person down the tunnel. He would get his Spencer carbine and head for the coulee overland. With luck, he'd be there to meet the small-footed person crawling out.

He left the house, then stopped, because the small-footed person had finished crawling through the tunnel and was coming back to the house.

"Hi," said Penny Winslow.

Torn raised an eyebrow. "You get around," he told her.

"I could say the same for you." Penny was still wearing Torn's black coat. She carried the Bulldog pistol in one hand and a lantern in the other. She was smeared with mud from the tunnel.

"Why'd you crawl through?" Torn said.

"I don't know," she said. "It was silly, I suppose, but I've been trained as a journalist to follow any lead."

"Find anything in there?"

She shook her head. "Just a lot of mud, and some rats' nests."

"Did you see who killed Larrabee?" Torn asked.

"No. I thought I heard a shot on my way here, but I can't be certain."

"How long have you been here?" Torn said.

"A half hour, I guess. I didn't see you coming. I must have been in the tunnel. Do you know why he was killed?"

Torn nodded. His voice was bitter. "He was killed to keep him from talking. He came to me before the army attacked the Indian camp. He said there was something he had to tell me. I was so worried about preventing a massacre that I didn't stop to listen. I told him I'd meet him here later."

Torn's eyes swept the Agency grounds, and the hills beyond. He detected no movement, no sign that Larrabee's killer was still in the area. Overhead, the gray clouds were shredding apart in angry swirls. Shafts of sunlight penetrated to the ground. "Why'd you come?" he asked Penny, as they started back into the house.

"For an interview, of course. I wanted to find out if what Standing Deer said about Larrabee was true. I figured I'd use my womanly wiles to squeeze the truth out of him."

Inside the house, Torn pointed to the trap door. "How'd you find the bolt hole?"

"I have a nose for these things," Penny said. "How do you think I escaped from the Sultan of Zanzibar?"

"I thought you escaped from slave dealers in Zanzibar," Torn said.

"In Zanzibar, it's the same thing."

Penny re-lit the lantern and slid into the bolt hole. "Look at this," she said. "Come on in."

Torn got into the hole beside her. Her body felt

warm against his in the cold dampness of the hole. The lantern cast an unearthly glow. She pulled a curved stick from the passageway. There was a small hole in the trapdoor, and she pushed the stick through. With the hook, she caught the carpet and dragged it over the trapdoor. "Clever, isn't it?"

They stayed like that a second, then she pushed the carpet back again. Torn opened the trap door, and they got out. Torn said, "That hole is fresh made. It's like Larrabee was expecting trouble. But was it trouble from Indians, or from somebody else?"

They searched the house. There wasn't much. Clothes belonging to Larrabee's family, who'd been sent from the Agency due to the threat of war. Under the bed in the back room, Clay found a strong box. He dragged it out. "Stand back," he told Penny.

With the .44, he shot the lock off the strongbox. The shot sounded loud in the small house. The smell of black powder was strong. He wondered if anybody had heard the shot.

Torn opened the strong box, and he and Penny rummaged through its contents. There were papers inside, legal documents. Underneath the papers were large bundles of Yankee greenbacks, neatly tied with string.

Torn thumbed through one of the bundles. "There's a small fortune here," he said. "A lot more than an Indian Agent makes."

The two of them went through the papers. There were legal documents relating to Larrabee's marriage. Sales receipts for Agency furnishing. Penny undid a pile of ribboned certificates.

"What's that?" Torn said.

Penny read the certificates. "They're shares," she said, and she looked up at Torn. "In the Prometheus Company."

"Do tell. What else do we have?" he looked at a document. "Here's a copy of the papers nominating Larrabee to be Indian agent." He read, then said, "Guess who his sponsor was?"

"Who?" she said.

"Cornelius Van Horne."

Torn pulled out some folders. "Here's the Agency receipts from last year."

He gave half of the folders to Penny, and they looked through them. There were weigh slips for cattle, and receipts for government pay vouchers issued the cattlemen. There were bound piles of ticket stubs. "The Indians turn these in when they receive their rations," Clay explained to Penny. "Each Indian is given a number to match the numbers printed on the tickets. That's how the government identifies them. Standing Deer, for example, is Red Hills 1."

Penny said, "That's sad, reducing them to numbers. They are people, after all."

Torn did some arithmetic. "According to these receipts, there were forty-five thousand pounds of beef given to the Indians for the winter. That should have been plenty to see them through." He rose. "Let's go down to the loading chutes and check the scales."

The cattle pen and adjacent weigh-chute were about half a mile from the Agency buildings. Torn and Penny took the horses. The sun was turning the snow to slush, and they did not feel like walking through it. Torn thought about taking Larrabee's coat, but it was too small for his broad shoulders.

As they rode, Penny said, "Don't you get cold in your shirt sleeves?"

"Yes," Torn told her, and he did not say any more.

They reached the cattle pen. It looked like it hadn't been used in a while. All the old droppings had been taken by the Indians and used for fuel. Torn and Penny tied their horses by the long chute, up which the cattle were prodded, to be branded, weighed and set aside for distribution.

Torn said, "On distribution day, the whole tribe gathers. The cattle are set loose on the prairie, and the men chase them with bows and spears. It's supposed to remind them of the old buffalo hunts. The Indians kill the cattle, then the women cut them up and carry them away. For accounting purposes, the meat is considered to have been distributed according to the agreed ration per person."

It took a few minutes to figure out how to work the big scale. When it read zero, Torn said to Penny, "Step on."

"Judge, you know a lady never reveals her weight," Penny said.

"Just this once," Torn said. "Do it for journalism."

Penny stepped on the scale.

The scale's arrow crept up the register. When it stopped, Torn said "You weigh . . . three hundred and twenty-eight pounds. No wonder you don't reveal it."

Penny stepped off the scale. "That means that instead of getting forty-five thousand pounds of beef for the winter, the Indians must really have gotten something closer to seventeen or eighteen thousand pounds."

Torn said, "Standing Deer was right. Larrabee *was* trying to starve the Indians into going to war. He was doing a good job, too. If the Cheyenne had to live on this beef ration, they'd never have made it through the winter."

"Maybe that's what Larrabee wanted to tell you," Penny said. "Maybe he felt guilty about what he was doing to the Indians, and he couldn't take it any more."

Torn shook his head. "There's more to this. Larrabee didn't get that much money from selling some Government cows for himself. You know, I think it's time to pay a visit to—"

He felt the bullet go by him before he heard the shot. "Get down," he told Penny, forcing her to her hands and knees in the cold slush. More bullets kicked in the snow. Bullets thunked the wood of the cattle pen. The shots were scattered. They came from a patch of woods at the bottom of a nearby hill.

"We can't stay here," Torn told Penny. "Run for it."

They untied the horses and got on. "Indians?" Penny said.

A bullet clipped Torn's saddle horn, just missing his hand. "They shoot too good to be Indians," he said.

They galloped for the agent's house. Ahead of them, a group of riders broke from the trees. They were white men, and in their lead was Pete Gallagher.

"They've got us cut off!" Torn yelled. "Make for the house."

Torn and Penny kicked in their heels. Their horses labored through the melting snow. Gallagher and his men were closer. Several fired pistols. Torn heard a ball whiz by.

Torn and Penny slid to a stop before the agent's house. Gallagher and his men were right behind. Penny jumped off her horse. Torn yanked the Spencer carbine from its bucket and dismounted, levering a shell into the chamber. Penny had the Bulldog out. She and Torn both fired at the oncoming riders. They fired again. One of the men swayed in the saddle, as the rest of the riders fired and turned away.

"Got him," Torn said.

"No, you didn't," Penny said. "I got him."

The riders dismounted in the coulee and opened fire on the house. Torn and Penny dashed inside.

Bullets crashed through the log walls, shattering the door, blowing out the window, gouging the walls, and splintering the furniture. Bullets broke lamps and thudded into Larrabee's body. Out front, Torn's horse ran off. Penny's horse was shot dead.

Penny spit out dust from all the splintered wood. "They're using up ammunition like somebody else is paying for it."

"Somebody else probably is," Torn said. He hugged the wall more tightly, as a bullet whined near his head. He looked out the window. "Here they come," he told Penny.

Gallagher and his men were coming for the house. They were spread out, firing on the move. "Get the woman alive," Gallagher yelled.

"Take the window," Torn told Penny.

Penny started shooting out the window. Torn ran out the door. He lay on the porch, taking careful aim, trying not to hurry, trying to make every bullet count. He had one magazine of seven shells for the Spencer, and ten bullets for the .44. He didn't know how many rounds Penny had for that British pistol, but it couldn't be a lot.

He squeezed off his shots. It was like the war. Swirling smoke. Yells, shots. Confusion. Fearing but not afraid, concentrating too hard to be truly scared. He saw figures fall in the snow, and then Gallagher's men were running away, back to the protection of the coulee. They left four of their company on the ground.

Torn went back in the house. Gallagher's men opened a steady fire on the building. A bullet splintered the door frame as Torn ducked back inside.

Torn's carbine was empty, and his spare ammunition had been lost when his horse ran away. He had six shots left for the .44. "How many rounds do you have?" he asked Penny.

She held up two fingers, flinching as a bullet struck nearby.

Torn looked at the sky. "It'll be dark before long. They'll rush us as soon as the light fades. At least we're lucky one way."

"What's that?" Penny said.

"They won't fire the house. You heard Gallagher—they want you alive."

"You mean, Murtaugh wants me alive," Penny corrected. "Honestly, his caveman approach is beginning to wear thin."

"They'll have to close on us," Torn said. "We won't be able to hold 'em off long, with eight bullets. We might not be able to hold them off at all."

Gallagher's men were spreading out of the coulee. They had the house under fire from three sides now. They were behind the barn and the shed. In a few minutes, the house would be surrounded.

Bullets hit all around Torn and Penny. Gallagher's men were working closer. It was almost dark.

"All right," Torn said. "Let's go."

CHAPTER

12

PENNY GRABBED THE LANTERN. TORN DREW UP
the rug and lifted the trap door. Penny climbed into
the hole first. Torn handed her the lantern, and she
lit it with a sulphur match. Torn climbed down with
her. They had to be careful not to set fire to themselves with the lamp in these close quarters. Torn
slid the stick through the hole in the trap door. He
closed the trap door, then dragged the rug over the
top of it.

"I'll go first," he said, taking the lantern.

He inched along the muddy tunnel, lantern in one
hand, pistol cocked and ready to fire in the other.
Penny followed him. The tunnel had been shored up
with timber. Crawling was difficult in the narrow
space. Torn and Penny were both breathing heavily.

The mud was cold and clammy.

"That trap door won't stop 'em for long," Torn said, puffing. "They'll find it and be right after us."

Penny said, "This is going to bring us out right in the middle of their positions, you know."

"Can't be helped."

From behind them, muffled sounds reverberated down the passage. Gallagher and his men must be in the house. Torn and Penny kept crawling. The breath rose faster in Torn's throat. He fought down a feeling of panic in the narrow tunnel. If they got trapped in here, they'd be helpless.

After what seemed an eternity, Torn sensed, rather than saw, a dim light ahead of him. He blew out the lantern. Carefully, so as not to make any noise, he and Penny crawled the remaining length of the passage.

The light became clearer. It was the faint glimmer of starlight, reflected off the snow. Clay felt the night air, fresh and cold on his face after the clamminess of the tunnel. The opening was small, barely large enough for a man to squeeze through. Torn peered out of it.

They were in the coulee. The sides were steep. There was brush around them, and rocks. He couldn't see much else. The tunnel opening was well screened. He strained his ears, but could hear nothing.

"Come on," he whispered to Penny.

Torn worked his way through the opening. Penny was right behind him. The ground was covered with freezing slush, which quickly soaked through their clothes. They knelt in the slush, listening, but there was no sound. In the tunnel behind them, they heard noise, distant exclamations.

Torn started to move, then stopped. He motioned for Penny to stop, too. He pointed.

Silhouetted against the horizon, not twenty yards away, were two men.

Noise could be heard from the agent's house now.

"What the hell are they yelling about?" one of the two men said.

"I don't know," said the second man. "I can't understand what . . ." He looked behind him suddenly.

"What is it?" said his partner.

"Huh? Thought I heard something. Must have been an animal."

Torn let out his breath. He motioned Penny forward. As he did, there were cries from the house, and the sound of men running their way.

"Bolt hole!" It was Gallagher's voice. "They got away! The opening is somewhere in this coulee. Spread out, and don't let them get past you."

The two guards began searching the side of the coulee, where Torn and Penny had been a moment before. Other men were doing the same. Then Gallagher was on the lip of the coulee, with the rest of his men. "Blackie and Cincinnati are in the tunnel. We'll catch Torn and the woman coming out this side."

Torn and Penny moved down the slope as quietly as they could. The slush crunched under their feet; their hands were raw and freezing. Torn realized that he still held the lantern. He couldn't let go of it now.

Behind them were low voices, as men searched

the hillside for the tunnel opening. Torn and Penny reached the bottom of the coulee. The chill wind froze their wet clothes to their skins. Their feet were club-like from the cold.

There was a shout, and Gallagher's two men emerged from the tunnel. "They ain't in there," yelled one.

Gallagher swore. "They can't have gone far. They got to be right around here. Spread out, boys, and find them. Remember—don't kill the woman."

Gallagher's men fanned out. Torn and Penny couldn't run for it. They'd be heard, then spotted immediately. There was some brush straight ahead, hidden in the shadow, and Torn led Penny into it. The short, sharp branches tore at their clothes and bodies. They wedged themselves into the darkest part.

Footsteps came toward them.

Torn and Penny tried to blend into the darkness. Penny was shivering, and Torn was afraid the noise of it would give them away. He put his arms around her, trying to warm her, trying not to shiver himself.

The footsteps were near. Dim shadows moved in front of the brush. These men were good. They weren't talking. They weren't making noise. One of them soundlessly poked the brush with his rifle barrel. The barrel stopped an inch from Torn's face. The man out there felt nothing, though. He withdrew the rifle barrel and moved on.

The footsteps faded. Torn held Penny tightly. She tried to relax against him, but she couldn't contain her violent shivering. Torn wasn't much better.

"We're safe for now," he said in a low voice. "But it won't last. When daylight comes, they'll have us dead. We've got to get to their horses."

"How do we do that?" Penny whispered.

Torn showed her the lantern. Stealthily, he rose from the brush and threw the lantern as far as he could up the coulee, in the opposite direction from the horses. The lantern bounced off some rocks, bounced again, then rattled noisily along the hillside. Somebody shot at it. The flash split the darkness. Other men began shooting at the flash.

"There they are!"

The rest of Murtaugh's men rushed toward the shooting. Footsteps passed the brush where Torn and Penny were hiding. When the footsteps were past, Torn led Penny out of the brush. They hurried down the coulee.

"Did you learn that trick in Charleston also?" Penny asked.

"No," Torn told her. "I read it in *Deadeye Dick's Daring Adventures*."

The horses were picketed further along the coulee. They were line-tied, still saddled. Torn didn't see a guard and there wasn't time to look for one.

Torn moved toward the horses, limping slightly in the cold. Penny followed, in the shadows. The horses smelled them coming, and stamped their hoofs and whinnied.

A figure loomed at Torn's side. "Pete, is that you? What the hell's going on up . . . ?"

Torn smashed the guard's head with his pistol. He felt bone crunch, and was sorry he had to do it. The guard cried once and dropped like a sack of rocks.

Torn started for the horses. There was movement behind him. A gunshot exploded. Torn heard a surprised gasp. He turned, in time to see a second guard drop his rifle and fall to the ground, cursing in pain. Penny caught up to Torn. He smelled the smoke from her pistol.

"Thanks," he said.

"Stop talking so much, and get the horses," she told him.

There were shouts from up the coulee, then a wild gunshot, followed by the sound of men running toward them. With his saber-knife, Torn cut two of the picketed horses free. Penny mounted one while Torn held the reins of the other, as he hacked through the picket ropes of the rest. Jumping on his own horse, he fired off the last rounds in his pistol, driving the freed horses down the coulee, toward the stream. Torn and Penny galloped after them.

Behind them were the frustrated curses of Gallagher and his men. There were gunshots, but in the darkness, Torn and Penny were almost impossible to hit.

They left the coulee at the stream, and started overland. When they had gone about a mile, they stopped and looked back. There was no sound. Nothing.

"We're not being followed," Torn said. "It'll be

hours before Gallagher and his men get their horses, if then."

"Now, then, what were you saying before we were interrupted?" Penny asked.

Torn sighed. "I don't suppose there's any chance of you letting me do this on my own?"

"None at all," she said.

"Then, I was saying—I think it's time to visit the Prometheus Company."

CHAPTER 13

LT. JAMES MCINTYRE, JIMMY TO HIS FRIENDS, waited with his patrol. They were just inside the Badlands. Before them was a pass through the fantastic maze of stone reefs and buttes that rose around them. It was a sterile, waterless land. It looked like another planet.

The patrol had been riding hard all day. A couple of hours ago, they had picked up the trail of about two dozen unshod ponies. Now they were waiting for their guide to return from scouting the pass. There had been no Crow scouts available to Jimmy, so he had picked up one of the Pine City Volunteers, a fellow named Duncan, said to have considerable experience in the country.

The pass was a good spot for an ambush, and

Jimmy didn't like going through. He had a bad feeling—not about Indians, he didn't think there were any Indians around—but there was something about this that wasn't right. He could not pinpoint it.

The afternoon sun shone through a watery sky. Behind Jimmy, Sgt. Reardon and the ten men of the patrol tried to stay warm. Their horses moved restlessly in the melted snow. The men wore their overcoats; their hats were pulled down. Walking their horses through the wet snow had given them all frozen feet. At the fort, they had fallen out in such a hurry that some of them—the newer men—had forgotten to take cold-weather clothing. Veterans, like Sgt. Reardon, wore enough extra layers for an expedition to the Arctic.

Their horses were still in good shape. Those of the Cheyenne must already be tired. The Indians' mounts had been half-starved even before the breakout. They wouldn't be able to match the cavalry's pace for long. Jimmy wanted to catch them before dark. He wanted to catch them before another patrol got to them, a patrol maybe led by an officer who would be less reluctant to shed blood than Jimmy. Jimmy was hoping that he could stop this war yet.

Duncan, lean and loose-limbed, picked his way back. He wore a moth-eaten buffalo robe coat, and he had a greasy, shifty look, but he had demonstrated his knowledge of the country.

Duncan reined in. "It's all clear, Lieutenant."

"You're sure?" Jimmy said.

"I'm sure, Lieutenant. I scouted all the way

through, and up the slopes. There's no Injuns within
five miles of here. I'd swear to it."

Jimmy hesitated.

Duncan said, "We got to hurry, Lieutenant, if we
want to catch them Injuns before dark."

Jimmy made up his mind. "Very well," he
said. He turned, "Sergeant. We'll proceed at a
quick walk, close intervals. Have the men keep a
sharp lookout."

Reardon, a big, red-headed fellow grinned. "Sir,
we always keep a sharp lookout."

Jimmy nodded to Duncan. The scout started back
into the pass. His horse's hoofs sounded loud on the
flinty ground.

"All right," Jimmy said. He motioned the patrol
forward. "Move out."

The soldiers started through the narrow pass.
The sides of the pass were steep. Great boul-
ders reared up, as if erupted from the depths of the
earth in some long-ago explosion. Here and there
the snow had melted to reveal patches of brown
earth.

Jimmy's eyes never stopped moving, never
stopped watching. Some of the soldiers had caught
his unease. They took their carbines from their
saddle sockets, and held them across their pom-
mels. Other men were bored or cold. Their minds
drifted to thoughts of home or the warmth of the
barracks.

The clop-clopping of the horses' hooves was loud
in the stillness of the pass. Bridle bits jingled. Brass
clinked.

The pass bent to the right. Duncan disappeared

around it. "Close up," Jimmy ordered.

The patrol rounded the bend. Up ahead, Duncan was waiting, watching them with a peculiar expression on his face. Jimmy's nose was running, like it always did in the cold. He wiped it for the hundredth time on the back of his serge coat sleeve.

The last of the soldiers was around the bend. Suddenly, Duncan turned his horse, whipped it and galloped away down the pass.

Jimmy said, "What . . . ?"

He heard a click.

He turned to his men. To warn them. He was too late. The sides of the pass exploded in an inferno of ear-shattering gunfire.

Jimmy saw men hit, saw them falling from their horses. Other men drew their weapons and looked for something to shoot at in the smoke and noise. Horses went down, screaming.

"Dismount!" Jimmy yelled. "Into the rocks. Let the horses go."

The men tried to obey. They scrambled from their horses, even as the bullets cut into them, knocked them down, chopped them to pieces. Sgt. Reardon fell, his head blown apart like a melon.

"Form a firing line!" Jimmy yelled. He led the survivors into the rocks. But too many men were falling too fast. The single-shot Springfields of the soldiers were no match for the Henrys and Winchesters of the attackers.

Jimmy McIntyre was the only man left on his feet. He fired his service revolver into the smoke and confusion. Then he saw his attackers advancing toward him. He recognized them, but before he had time to be surprised, he was dead.

By then, the attackers' knives were already at work on the bodies of the soldiers.

CHAPTER

14

TORN AND PENNY LEARNED ABOUT THE MAS-
sacre while they were riding to Pine City. They were
overtaken by a courier sent from Major Darcy to
Fort Connor. The courier, a corporal, slowed enough
to tell them that an army patrol had been ambushed
and wiped out.

"It happened just inside the Badlands," the courier
said, "in Frenchman's Pass. So keep your eyes
peeled. You're likely to encounter hostiles anywhere
around here."

The courier galloped on. Torn looked toward Pine
City, then he looked west, past Council Butte, to
the Badlands.

Penny anticipated him. "I guess the Prometheus
Company will have to wait."

"I guess," Torn replied.

They rode toward the Badlands. Torn had been in this country before. He knew Frenchman's Pass. The sun was out, and it felt good, as it melted the rest of the snow and partially thawed their frozen bodies.

They arrived at the massacre site. Major Darcy and Captain Harman were already there, with a small party of men. The bodies of the dead soldiers had been laid in a row. They were covered by gray army blankets. Blood showed through some of the blankets, bare feet stuck out of others. The ambushed patrol's horses had been run off. Cheyenne arrows were scattered among the rocks.

The young soldiers of Darcy's detail were shaken by what had happened, and outraged. One of them sat off by himself, crying. Darcy himself paced back and forth in a cold rage. His polished boots gleamed in the sunlight. When he saw Torn, he stopped pacing, and sneered. "You're too late to save your Indian friends this time, Torn. When I find them, they're dead. All of them. Look what they've done to my boys. Go ahead, look."

"It's best you don't see this," Torn told Penny, and she backed her horse away.

Torn dismounted. A battered campaign hat had been placed atop one of the blanketed bodies. Clay thought he recognized the hat. He lifted one edge of the blanket.

Jimmy McIntyre was naked. He had been scalped, and his body had been cut apart in the most hideous manner. His head had been half severed from his shoulders, and it lolled at an odd angle. He stared sightlessly, a spectral grin on his face.

Torn replaced the blanket. You won't be getting any fancy cigars now, he thought grimly.

"Satisfied?" Darcy said. It was an accusation. "If I had attacked the Cheyenne when I wanted, these men would still be alive. You should be ashamed to show yourself here, Torn. And you, Miss Winslow, should be ashamed to be seen with him."

Penny stiffened in the saddle. "I'll be the judge of whom I'm seen with, Major Darcy."

Darcy turned away in disgust.

Captain Harman beckoned Torn and Penny over. He took in their mud-caked, bedraggled appearance, their ripped clothing. "Where have you two been? What's happened to you? You look frozen. Sgt. Preston—get my overcoat from my horse and give it to Miss Winslow, please."

"Yes, sir," said the sergeant.

"We've been at the Agency," Torn said. "Larrabee's dead. He was killed by Pete Gallagher and some of his men. They almost got us, too."

"Why would Pete Gallagher kill Larrabee?" Harman wanted to know.

"Because Standing Deer was right. Larrabee was starving them. He was weighing the cattle rations heavy, and selling the rest on the side. He was going to tell me about it, but Gallagher got to him first."

The overcoat came. Penny gave Torn back his suit jacket and put on the heavy blue coat.

"Don't say anything about this, just yet," Torn told Harman.

"All right." Harman led the two of them to where some soldiers had a small fire going, with coffee brewing in a gallon tin. "Do you drink coffee, Miss Winslow?" the captain said.

"Right now, I'll drink anything, as long as it's hot," Penny replied.

"Give them each a cup," Harman told the soldier tending the fire. The soldier's face betrayed his reluctance to give coffee to the man accused of causing the deaths of his comrades, but did as he was ordered.

Torn and Penny sipped the scalding coffee. Torn felt its warmth circulating through his stomach and into his body. "Did they get everyone in the patrol?" he asked Harman.

Harman shook his head. "The guide is missing. He was one of Murtaugh's men, name of Duncan. He must have escaped. That, or the Cheyenne took him prisoner, poor fellow. One of our Pawnee scouts found the bodies. The rest of the battalion is back at Standing Deer's old camp."

There was the sound of hoofbeats. A trooper rounded the bend of the narrow pass. The soldiers waiting there got out of his way.

The soldier reined in before Major Darcy and saluted. "Captain Yates sends his compliments, sir. Lieutenant Gibson's patrol has found the Cheyenne trail. They crossed it about ten miles north of the battalion position. It's a big trail, sir. The whole tribe. They're headed due north."

"Deeper into the hills," Darcy said. He turned to Harman. "You were right, Captain. Standing Deer is going to make a stand." He smacked a gauntleted fist into his palm, grinning in triumph. "We've got him." Then he said, "Lieutenant DeRudio."

"Sir," replied the patrol commander.

"Detail five men to wait here for the horses from the fort and help get these bodies back. Have this courier be one of them, so that he can rest his mount."

"Yes, sir."

"Get the rest of the men ready to move out."

"Yes, sir," said the lieutenant, who turned, calling for his sergeant.

Next, Darcy said, "Orderly."

"Here, sir," said a trooper, stepping forward.

"Ride to the battalion as fast as you can. My compliments to Captain Yates, and he's to have the men ready to march immediately on my return."

"Yes, sir." The orderly saluted. He mounted his horse and clattered out of the pass.

"Aren't you going to follow the tracks of the killers?" Torn asked.

"Why?" said Darcy. His eyes shone. He was going to get his battle. "It would be a waste of time. This was the work of a raiding party. The Indians who committed this atrocity will be back with the main body by now."

"You don't . . ." Torn said.

"When I need suggestions from you, Judge, I'll ask for them. And, take my word on it, that day will be a long time coming. Now get out of my way. I have an Indian war to fight."

While the soldiers prepared to move out, Torn said to Penny. "Just for fun, let's you and I see if we can't find the killers' tracks and follow them ourselves."

Penny looked a bit puzzled, but she went along

with him. The soldiers formed up and marched out of the pass. Torn and Penny rode the other way.

The army horses had been run out of the pass. At the end of the pass, their tracks merged with those of the killers.

Torn dismounted and examined the tracks. "They were picked up by about two dozen men, riding unshod horses. Well, well, where have we seen that before?"

He remounted. Penny said, "They certainly didn't make any attempt to hide their trail. It's like they weren't worried about pursuit. What happened to the scout—what was his name—Duncan?"

"There's no sign of him. He either vanished into thin air, or his tracks are mixed in with these."

"He's a prisoner?"

"Maybe."

"What do you mean, maybe?" Penny said. "What else could he be?"

"We'll see," Torn said. "The killers' horses are bigger and healthier than any I saw in Standing Deer's camp. They've been fed more grain than Indian horses, too, even reservation Indians."

"Are you saying what I think you're saying?"

"We'll know soon enough," Torn replied.

They followed the trail of the killers and stolen horses. Almost immediately, the trail turned southwest, coming down out of the Badlands and onto the prairie, the opposite direction from that taken by the main band of Cheyenne. Torn and Penny were soon able to follow it at a steady lope. Evening came, and they saw a faint glow on the horizon.

"That's Pine City," Penny said. "The tracks are headed into town."

"That's right," Torn said. "Cheyenne didn't murder those soldiers. White men did."

CHAPTER 15

IT WAS NIGHT WHEN TORN AND PENNY SNUCK into Pine City.

They had waited for darkness, not wanting to be seen; Pine City had not been the most hospitable environment for them. They had lost track of the men they were following, but that was to be expected. The killers' tracks had faded into the thousands of tracks on the rutted road leading into town. It was enough to know that Lt. McIntyre and his patrol had been killed by white men.

Torn and Penny approached the picket house that served as headquarters for the Prometheus Company. They felt their way in the dark. Behind them, there was music and laughter and lights from the saloons on Main Street.

It had turned cold. The street was a icy morass from the melted snow. Torn's boots squelched in the sucking mud; Penny's feet were freezing, though she didn't complain. "We'll be lucky if we don't die from pneumonia," Torn muttered, wearing only his black suit coat.

Torn carried an unlit lantern he'd stolen from a stable near where they'd left their horses. Penny had the Bulldog pistol with its two rounds; she still wore Captain Harman's blue greatcoat.

Behind the company office was a large, almost endless yard. There were rows of transport, and canvas-covered piles of equipment. Torn and Penny crept into the yard.

Suddenly Torn raised a hand. They stopped.

A watchman was making his rounds, coming toward them.

The guard was only half paying attention to what he was doing. He wasn't expecting trouble. Torn thought about hitting him with his pistol, but he didn't want to kill him. He and Penny waited, shivering in the cold, until the watchman got close. As he came by, Torn stepped out of the shadows and hit him in the jaw with a terrific overhand right. The watchman grunted and crumpled to the ground. Torn tied the man's hands and gagged him with a strip of cloth ripped from his shirt. He sat the man against a wagon wheel; the man's head hung to one side.

"Do you realize how many times you've broken the law in the last few days, Judge?" Penny asked.

"I know," Torn responded. "There's times I feel like swearing out a warrant against myself."

They scurried to one of the huge, canvas-covered mounds. Torn worked loose one of the grommets and lifted an edge of the stiff canvas. He felt around inside. He touched metal, hard edges.

"Machinery," he whispered to Penny. "No way of telling what it is."

Penny looked around. "There's enough wagons here to transport an army."

Torn nodded. "Whatever they're up to, it's big."

They left the yard and went to the company office. The picket house was not well constructed. On the door was a hand-lettered sign: "We don't keep cash. Rob somebody else." The door was fastened by a simple rope latch. Torn opened it, and they went in.

Inside, it was pitch black. The house smelled of dust and stale cigar smoke. The packed dirt floor was muddy from the weather. Torn raised a panel of the dark lantern, struck a match and lit it. The lantern's three closed panels would keep the light from showing too much—or so he hoped.

Torn looked around. There was a desk, some crates used for chairs, a crude table. In one corner was a small safe. On the desk were some ledgers. He opened one.

"Pay receipts for the men here," he said, flipping through. "They're spending forty dollars a week on . . . seven hundred and some men. About twelve thousand dollars a month."

The other ledgers contained inventories of animals and transport owned by the company. "They have a fortune invested here," Torn said. "This is no run-of-the-mill land development company."

He squatted and looked at the safe. It was made of thick steel, with a combination lock.

"I don't want to shoot off the lock," he said. "It would make too much noise." He put his arms around the safe. "Too heavy to lift." He shook his head, "We'll have to take the chance. Hand me that British pistol."

"You can't shoot off a lock like this," Penny told him. "Hold the lantern."

Torn looked at her, surprised. She knelt beside the safe. She put an ear to the combination. She turned the knob, slowly, listening for the fall of the tumblers. "Hold the light closer," she said.

He did as he was told. "Don't tell me you learned this from the Sultan of Zanzibar," he said.

"Heavens, no," Penny said. "Otto von Bismarck taught me, over the course of a long, rainy day. Otto considers this sort of thing an intellectual exercise. He would have made a wonderful criminal."

Penny heard the last tumblers fall. She gave the safe's handle a jerk, and the door swung open.

"You might have made a pretty good criminal, yourself," Torn told her.

He knelt, holding the lantern close. Inside the safe were three folders. Nothing else.

"They're right about one thing," Penny said. "There's no cash. They must bring it in for paydays."

Torn pulled out the folders and set them on the table. He opened the first one.

"It's an assay report," he said. "Delivered to J. Murtaugh, et al."

They looked at each other. "Now we know who the Prometheus Company is," Penny said.

Torn read from the report, "'A claim located in Dakota Territory, near the area known as the Devil's Punchbowl, on a tract of land not more than five hundred yards from... et cetera, et cetera.'" He read on silently for a moment, then said, "We also know why Murtaugh wants the Red Hills. It's not for farmers, and it's not for cattle. It's for mining."

"Gold?" Penny said.

Torn shook his head. "Copper. If I read this report right, the Red Hills are a solid mass of it, maybe the biggest lode ever discovered in this country. That's what gives the hills their color, the copper ore. Murtaugh went in there last year, in violation of the treaty, and brought out his own ore samples. 'The others' that Runs With the Wind talked about must have been Murtaugh and his party."

He opened the next folder.

"It's a map," Penny said.

Torn spread out the heavy paper, folding the creases smooth. "My God, look at this."

A portion of the Red Hills had been reproduced to the last detail and gridded. Torn said, "Murtaugh must have had surveyors in there with him. Look, they've drawn a stamping mill near the Devil's Punchbowl."

"That's what the machinery is for, out back," Penny said.

Torn tapped the map. "They've got roads penciled

in, a railroad line, even a town."

"They thought of everything," Penny said.

"They seem confident of getting it, too," Torn replied.

He opened the third folder. "It's a town plat. They've formed a company under the Townsite Act."

"Let me guess," Penny said. "The Prometheus Company."

Torn nodded. "They've claimed three hundred and twenty acres outside the Devil's Punchbowl. The land's been divided into lots 125 feet by 25. Members of the company can buy the lots for $1.25 an acre, then sell or rent them for whatever the market will bear."

"And with the richness of those copper veins, that will be a lot," Penny said.

"It's a license to print money." Torn's mouth formed a grim smile. "Look at the names on the town lots—Stephen A. Darcy, Cornelius Van Horne, Amos Larrabee. There's a couple more I don't know, probably people connected with the railroad."

"That's how Murtaugh got their cooperation," Penny said. "He's going to make them all rich."

"And himself even richer than he already is. Some people are never satisfied. The Devil's Punchbowl is the Cheyennes' most sacred ground. Murtaugh knew they'd never lease it or give it up voluntarily, so they had to be swindled out of it."

Penny said, "Larrabee and Darcy would start an Indian war, and with Van Horne handling things in

Washington, all they had to do was sit back and start counting the money."

Torn stuck the folders inside his shirt. "They won't be counting any money if I can help it," he said. "Come on."

CHAPTER 16

CORNELIUS VAN HORNE'S SPACIOUS TENT LAY
at the end of town, surrounded by the less imposing
quarters of his staffers. It was an old army headquarters tent, with a covered entrance-way. Inside,
there was a Sibley stove for warmth. The camp bed
was covered with furs, and buffalo skins served as
rugs on the earth floor.

Van Horne's mistress, Seneca, sat on the bed with
a blanket wrapped around her. Lustrous, raven-black
hair cascaded onto her creamy shoulders, which
gleamed in the guttering light of the lamp. She had
pouty lips and eyes like pools of dark liquid. The
velvet dress that she'd worn earlier lay thrown care-
lessly across her trunk.

Van Horne, wearing a thick robe, filled two glasses

from an iced bottle of champagne. His own clothes were folded neatly on a camp chair. He carried the glasses back to the bed. His bony feet squished mud beneath the buffalo skin rugs. "God, I hate these fact-finding missions," he said in his clipped New England accent. "Conditions here are so primitive. I wish we could have stayed back in Sioux City, in that special car that the President of the Northern Railroad lent us. At least it had a real floor."

He sat beside Seneca, running a finger along her bare shoulder. "I can't wait to get back to Washington. The trappings of civilization will seem all the more delicious after this experience."

"I don't know," Seneca said, with an accent that held more than a trace of the Old South. "I rather like it here. People treat me like a real lady—the way they used to treat me, when I was on the stage and they were calling me the next Lola Montez. Why, when I go out on what passes for a street here, men actually tip their hats. Plus, we don't have to worry about your wife breaking in on us. You know, a couple times it has gotten rather dicey, Corney, dear."

From the darkness of the entrance way, came a chuckle. "Corney?"

Seneca gasped. Van Horne whirled, spilling his champagne. Two figures detached themselves from the shadows. One was tall and lean; the other shorter, wearing an army greatcoat.

"Judge Torn," said Van Horne in surprise. "Miss Winslow."

Torn held Penny's Bulldog pistol on the congressman. Seneca's eyes roamed over Torn's rugged figure with undisguised approval. To Penny she said,

"Are you Penelope Winslow? I heard you were in town. I always wanted to meet you. You're one of the few women I know who's caused more scandal than me."

"Sorry to interrupt your paperwork, Congressman," Torn said.

Van Horne stiffened and cleared his throat, "I assure you, this isn't what it..."

"I want you to tell me who killed those soldiers," Torn said.

"Why, Indians did it," Van Horne said. "Everybody knows..."

"I don't have time for lies, Congressman. White men killed those soldiers, and I want to know who they were."

"I...I have no idea. Really, I..."

"Was it you?" Torn asked.

"No. No, of course not. I..."

"No, you don't have the guts," Torn said. "But you know who did it. And you're going to tell me who it was."

Terror showed on Van Horne's bird-like features. "Please, I swear to you. I don't know. Listen, Judge, it's not too late to come to an arrangement, you know. I have nothing against you personally. I only voted against your nomination on principle. I..."

With one hand, Torn grabbed the velvet lapels of Van Horne's robe. With the other, he shoved the Bulldog pistol under the lawmaker's nose. "You tell me who killed those soldiers, or I'll splatter your brains over this tent." He shook Van Horne until the congressman's teeth knocked together. "Who was it? Was it Pete Gallagher?"

"It was me," said Jim Murtaugh.

Torn and Penny turned. Murtaugh held a pistol on them. Pete Gallagher was beside Murtaugh, with his new Winchester. There was a third man with them, a shifty-looking man in a moth-eaten buffalo coat, holding a Sharps carbine.

Murtaugh said, "Drop the pistol, Judge."

Torn did.

Penny took a step back involuntarily. Murtaugh scared her. Seneca put down her champagne. The man in the moth-eaten coat was staring at her. He was practically drooling, and she drew the blanket high around her naked shoulders.

Van Horne said, "I don't want trouble here, Murtaugh. I've got a . . ."

"Be quiet," Murtaugh told him.

The congressman swallowed.

Murtaugh smiled at Torn, a hard smile. "Normally Pete would have been the one to take care of those soldiers," he explained. "But I'd already sent him to deal with Larrabee. So I took our little band of 'Indians,' and I did the job myself. We made it look very realistic, if I do say so."

Van Horne said, "Larrabee? What happened to Larrabee? You mean, he's . . . dead?"

"As a coffin nail," Murtaugh said. "His conscience got to him. He was going to tell the judge everything. I'm going to give Mr. Duncan here Larrabee's shares in the new town lots. I'd make Duncan the new Indian agent, too, except there's not going to be any more Indians when Darcy gets finished with them."

The three men laughed. To Torn, Murtaugh said,

"Gallagher told me how you and Miss Winslow had gotten away from him. When we came back to town and found our offices ransacked, I figured we'd find you here."

Torn said, "Gallagher and his men, they've been the ones running off stock, right? Dressing up like Indians, letting themselves be seen, but always at a distance?"

Murtaugh grinned. "That's right, Judge."

"They're the ones that tried to kill me that first day, too, I suppose."

"Right again. We were going to use your death to start our Indian war. If that didn't work, Darcy and the others at the agency were going to fake an attack on themselves, and start the war that way, but you spoiled that, too."

"Who burned the Agency?"

"Larrabee," Murtaugh said. "The drunken fool was a day early. He didn't give us time to hang you—or maybe that was his reason. Too bad about Larrabee. He did good work for us, till he started getting cold feet about what was going to happen to his Indian friends."

"Told you we shouldn't have picked no squaw lover for that job," said Pete Gallagher.

Duncan chortled, still looking at Seneca. "He ain't loving squaws no more."

"Is one mine worth so many dead men?" Torn asked.

Murtaugh laughed. "You don't know half of it. The Prometheus Company is going to control the entire Red Hills reservation. Not just the mine. Once the land is declared public domain, the settlers will come.

Half will fail the first year, and the company will buy them out for next to nothing. The rest we'll pressure to sell—and you know how good we can be at that. We'll resell their properties as improved sites and charge what we want for them. We'll own the towns, the transportation. We'll own half this territory."

"You think of everything, don't you?" Torn asked.

"Actually, I didn't think of it. It was Darcy."

"Darcy?"

"Yeah. Funny, ain't it? I've never known a soldier to have that kind of brains. Or any brains at all, when it comes to it. Darcy came to me with the idea. He thought there might be minerals on the reservation land. Every step of the way, it's been Darcy in the lead. He needs money bad, you see. His wife is a big spender, and he has to keep up with the swells in that tin soldier regiment of his. There was never any danger the Indians would be relocated, either. Darcy is determined to have his war. He wants to get his name in the papers, be a big hero. Me, I'm happy with the money."

"Whose idea was it to ambush that patrol?" Torn asked.

"Darcy's."

Torn's throat felt like it had been rubbed with sandpaper. "His own men?"

Murtaugh shrugged. "Soldiers are expendable. It was in the public interest, after all.

"Enough talk, Judge. The Indians have one last outrage to commit. It's going to be a shame how they caught you riding by yourself."

Alarmed, Seneca said, "Cornelius, can't you do something about this?"

Van Horne cleared his throat, stiffening. "Afraid not, my dear. It's the way things are settled out here."

"That's right, Congressman. If you want your re-election money, you be a good boy," Murtaugh said.

Seneca was repelled. Van Horne attempted to put a comforting arm around her shoulder, but she shied away from him.

Murtaugh turned. "Miss Winslow, you have a choice. You can end up with the judge here—by the way, you know what Indians do to women before they kill them, don't you?"

Penny went pale. Gallagher grinned. Duncan's small eyes were alight with anticipation.

Murtaugh went on. "Or, you can come with me. Winter's almost here, and I need somebody to keep me warm. It's up to you. Come with me and live. Or go with the judge and die."

Penny tried to keep from trembling. Murtaugh smiled at her. "You see, Miss Winslow, I win in the end. I always do."

Penny said, "What . . . what about my story?"

"Oh, you'll get to write it. You'll have to change it around a bit, but don't worry, I'll treat you good. After all, you're a public figure." He chuckled, "We'll be quite a couple, the Copper King and the Scandal Queen. Now, what's it to be?"

Penny licked her lips. She glanced from Murtaugh to Torn. There was a pleading look on her face. "I don't want to die, Judge. Not that way. You understand, don't you?"

"Sure," said Torn. "I understand."

Penny hesitated. She lowered her eyes, ashamed.

"I'm sorry," she told Torn in a low voice. She stepped across the tent and stood beside Murtaugh, linking an arm through his. She looked into Murtaugh's eyes and smiled. He smiled back. The two of them understood each other. Gallagher and Duncan looked disappointed.

"All right, Judge," said Murtaugh. "Let's take a walk."

Pete Gallagher said, "You gonna let me kill him?"

Murtaugh felt his face, which was still bruised and swollen from his fight with Torn. "No. I'll do this myself."

Penny was hanging onto Murtaugh's arm. Suddenly, she jerked the arm down and shoved Murtaugh sideways. At the same time, she turned and threw herself into Gallagher, knocking him off balance. Gallagher's Winchester went off.

Torn made a rolling dive for the British pistol. Duncan fired at him but missed.

Torn retrieved the pistol and came up on one knee. There were two shots left. He fired the pistol at Murtaugh, hitting him an instant before the man fired his own pistol, making Murtaugh's shot go wide. Gallagher had levered his Winchester and was aiming it. Torn fired again. The bullet hit Gallagher square in the chest, knocking him onto his back. Duncan dropped his rifle and turned to run. Torn pulled out his saber-knife, aimed it and threw. The blade caught Duncan in the back, between the shoulder blades. Duncan stopped with a strangled cry. His hands flailed futilely as he tried to withdraw the blade. He staggered backwards, then sideways, and fell into the Sibley stove, knocking open the grate.

Torn got to his feet, breathing hard. Powder smoke filled the tent. It seemed suddenly quiet after the noise of the gunshots. Murtaugh and his men were dead. Outside, there were shouts, the sound of running feet.

Torn looked at Penny. "For a minute, there, I thought you were going to go with him."

Penny grinned. "Being able to lie well is an essential tool of journalism."

Glowing coals had spilled from the stove onto Duncan's body. Torn stamped them out. He withdrew his saber-knife from Duncan's back. "Poor fellow got all burned up over this," he said. He took Van Horne's white shirt from the camp chair, and cleaned the knife's blade on it.

Congressman Van Horne had retreated to the far side of the tent. His pale face had grown even paler. His eyes were wide with fear. Seneca, still wrapped in the blanket, regarded Torn and Penny with admiration. She said. "That was nice work, you two. If either of you are ever in Washington, and you need a place to stay . . ."

"Seneca!" said Van Horne.

Torn looked at the ex-dancer, and a corner of his mouth turned up in smile. "I'll keep that in mind, ma'am."

He picked up Van Horne's fur overcoat and put it on.

"Hey," said Van Horne, "you can't take that."

Torn ignored him. He handed Penny the Bulldog pistol and took Gallagher's pistol and shell belt, along with the Winchester repeater. Penny took Duncan's rifle, and the two of them started from the tent.

Van Horne said, "What about these bodies? What am I supposed to do with them?"

"Write your congressman," Clay told him. "There ought to be a law against this sort of thing."

He and Penny went out.

CHAPTER 17

MAJOR DARCY SURVEYED THE SCENE BELOW him with his field glasses. The rest of his officers stood nearby, doing the same. Behind them, the four troops of cavalry were dismounted, waiting, along with what was left of the Pine City Volunteers. They had been riding most of the night. Men and horses were tired, but not too tired to fight.

It was mid-morning, a fair, cold day. They were deep in the Red Hills. Before them was an area known as the Devil's Punchbowl, an enormous hollow in the earth, surrounded on three sides by towering crags of rock. Standing Deer had withdrawn his people into this vast, crater-like depression. From the height on which they stood, Darcy and the others could see Indian horses on the inner slopes of the

143

Punchbowl. They saw women and children milling
about. There were no warriors visible. The terrain
between the heights and the Punchbowl was fairly
level. Patches of snow remained in the rocks and
other shady spots where the sun did not get through.

"Standing Deer is your typical stupid Indian,"
Darcy said. "Any schoolboy knows you take the high
ground, not the low. If we had a couple of howitzers
we could lob shells in on them till there was no one
left."

"But we don't have any howitzers," said Captain
Harman, lowering his field glasses. "You could never
bring artillery through these passes, anyway."

"That's all right, it would save us the fun of doing
this ourselves. If this is where the Cheyenne want
to die, I'm happy to oblige them. It makes our job
that much easier."

Darcy put the glasses down. He stroked his waxed
moustache. The chill breeze ruffled the havelock on
his kepi. The assembled officers waited for his word.
He liked that. He liked the feeling of power.

"Well," Darcy told Captain Harman, "your Indian
friends have led us an interesting chase, with some
luck and a lot of help from the weather. But it ends
here. Now they learn how the Seventh Cavalry av-
enges its dead. I've been waiting for this day a long
time."

He slid his field glasses back into their polished
leather case. "We attack right away."

"You won't give them a chance to surrender?"
Harman said.

Darcy looked at his adjutant with disapproval.
"Afraid some of them might get killed?"

Harman stiffened. "Perhaps, sir. Perhaps I don't want to see our men killed, either."

"I think our men are ready to take their chances, Captain. That's what soldiering is about, in case you had forgotten. The enemy is to receive no quarter. Remember Lt. McIntyre and his men. Women and children will be treated as hostile."

"Sir, I must protest," Harman said.

"Your protest is noted, Captain. You may stay here, with the reserve."

Harman took in his breath. He said nothing.

Darcy went on, addressing the other officers. "There will be no surprises this time, gentlemen. This time, the Indians are there. We'll attack in line. H Company on the left, I in the middle, L on the right with the rest of these civilian Volunteers. K Company will be in reserve, with the pack train. Each man will carry one hundred rounds of carbine ammunition, twenty-four rounds for pistol. They'll leave their overcoats with the pack train. We move out in ten minutes. Any questions?"

There were none.

Darcy turned to Harman. "Questions, Captain?"

"A lot of questions, sir, but I doubt there would be many satisfactory answers."

Darcy smiled thinly. "Very well, gentlemen, join your troops."

The officers returned to their companies. Sergeants gave orders in sharp tones. The men checked their weapons. They lined up their rolled overcoats by the pack train. Saddle girths were tightened. Hats were pulled low. Carbine slings were adjusted, pistols loosened in their holsters. Men grabbed a last bite of hardtack. They took a last drink from their canteens.

Harman dismounted the reserve company and positioned them on the heights, where they'd be ready to back up the attack, if needed. Some of the officers with the attacking companies made a point of shaking his hand before they left.

"Prepare to mount." The order went down the column.

"Mount."

As one, the soldiers swung into their saddles. Carbine barrels were inserted in saddle sockets. Behind them, the civilians mounted in ragged fashion.

"By two's. Forward, march."

The three companies of cavalry, a hundred and fifty men, filed over the crest and down from the height. There was the jingling of bits, the crunching of hooves on rock. The men were tense, as they always were when going into action. In the rear, the civilians were louder. Some were joking. A few looked drunk.

Captain Harman stood on the heights with the officers of K Company. Through their field glasses, they watched the attacking troops reach the canyon floor and form line, with the civilians bunched on the far right.

A bugle sounded the advance. There was no need for quiet, the Indians knew where they were. The line moved forward. There was no sign of activity in the Punchbowl.

Darcy motioned with his arm. The line gathered speed. There was no dust. The ground was soupy mud from the melted snow. Harman saw Major

Darcy out front, sitting his black charger like he was on parade. There was movement in the Punchbowl now, as women and children were sent to the bottom of the depression with the horses.

Faster went the soldiers, a brisk canter now. The line was holding well. On the right, the civilians were predictably ragged.

From the front of the line sounded the thin notes of the Charge.

At once the line bounded forward, the men yelling, waving their pistols, their screams thin and high-pitched at this distance, carried on the breeze.

The line grew ragged, as the faster horses surged in front. Hats blew off. Men were straining to be first into the Punchbowl.

They were close now. Men rose in their saddles. Darcy was waving his pistol.

From the rim of the Punchbowl, Harman saw puffs of smoke. A fraction of a second later, he heard the gunshots. A continuous, rolling volley. The front rank of soldiers disappeared into the smoke. Saddles were emptied. Men and horses went down in a confused, yelling mass. The soldiers pressed on, but the gunfire was too intense, too accurate. The line was brought up short of the rim. Horses reared. The soldiers were firing back now, using their pistols. More men fell, troops and civilians, toppling into the mud. Others, caught in their stirrups, were dragged along by maddened horses.

Harman bit his lip. Those were his men, his friends, being shot to pieces.

Miraculously, Darcy was untouched. Harman

saw him waving his arm. At Darcy's command, the
troops split up. They made for the cover of the
rocks on either side of the Punchbowl, where they
dismounted. As horse-holders took the mounts
to the rear, the rest of the men opened a steady
carbine fire on the unseen Indians at the lip of
the depression.

The Indian fire slackened. In front of the Punchbowl, the smoke cleared. Harman saw dead men and
horses. He saw wounded men crawling through the
mud to cover. Other wounded men and horses were
thrashing and crying in pain. Riderless mounts galloped over the canyon.

There was a bitter taste in Harman's mouth. He
felt nauseated. He realized how much he hated war.

From the rocks, soldiers started forward again,
singly and in small groups. The Indians at the lip of
the Punchbowl began firing once more. Men crumpled. Others fell to the ground and fired from where
they were, or sought cover back in the rocks or
behind the bodies of the dead.

Harman had to admire Standing Deer. The Cheyenne chief had made use of the terrain and the
soldiers' natural eagerness to attack to give
them a bloodying. Harman felt his sympathies
strangely divided. He almost cheered for the
Indians, but he couldn't go against his own comrades.
He had to hope the soldiers would win. And they
would. With the Indians' old weapons and scarcity of
ammunition, the end was inevitable. They were just
putting it off.

The Cheyenne fire was lessening again. They
were saving their bullets for the final charge. Stand-

ing Deer had instilled in them a discipline rarely known among Indians.

Through his glasses, Harman saw an Indian bound over the lip of the Punchbowl, carrying a coup stick. It was Gray Thunder, Standing Deer's son-in-law. Gray Thunder dashed forward into the smoke and mud to count coup, and in that one gesture Harman seemed to see the whole tragedy of the Indian wars, Stone Age men trying to touch the bodies of modern soldiers, a prehistoric challenge to progress, a last defiant gesture to civilization.

Gray Thunder ran toward a wounded officer. Harman recognized Lt. Varnum of H Company. Gray Thunder raised his coup stick. As he did, Varnum lifted himself off the ground and fired his pistol. Gray Thunder flung up his arms and fell. He started to crawl away, and Harman lost sight of him in the swirling wreaths of powder smoke.

The soldiers and few civilians who were left began advancing again, foot by foot, firing as they went. They laid down a covering fire on the lip of the Punchbowl. Mud spurted where bullets hit. There was no return fire. Darcy and the surviving officers led the men forward in a rush. As the first soldiers reached the lip of the depression, shots rang out. Men spun and dropped. Others dove for cover. Once again Standing Deer had outthought them. He'd withdrawn to the bottom of the Punchbowl. As the advancing soldiers reached the lip of the depression, they made perfect targets against the skyline.

More men were moving forward now. The Indians' ammunition must be nearly gone. The end was just a matter of time. Harman wondered if his reserve troop would be called upon to help in the slaughter that must ensue. He prayed that they wouldn't be.

Behind him were hoofbeats. He turned. It was Judge Torn and that Winslow woman, riding hard.

CHAPTER 18

TORN SLID HIS LATHERED HORSE TO A HALT and dismounted. Penny was right behind him. She dismounted as well. The other officers of K Company turned to them.

Torn glanced off the height, at the battle around the Punchbowl. "Call off the attack," he told Harman.

"I wish I could," said the captain.

"You can. Lt. McIntyre and his men weren't killed by Indians. Jim Murtaugh did it—at Major Darcy's instigation."

"What!" said Harman. "That's insane. Can you prove that?"

"Murtaugh told me. Miss Winslow was a witness. So were Congressman Van Horne and his girl friend. This Indian war was a put-up job from the start."

Harman seemed dazed. "But . . . why?"

"Money and glory," Torn said. He reached into his shirt and pulled out the Prometheus Company's folders. "Read these."

Harman took the folders. He read the assay report. He looked at the map of the Red Hills and the town plat. In the background, the gunfire took on a new urgency. Torn tapped a foot impatiently.

When Harman was done, he put down the folders. "Trumpeter!" he called.

The company bugler stepped forward.

"Sound Recall," Harman ordered. "Keep sounding it until the battalion returns."

The soldier looked confused. "Sir . . . ?"

"You heard me," Harman snapped.

The trumpeter glanced at his comrades, then he said, "Yes, sir."

The trumpeter stood on the crest of the height. He raised the bugle to his lips. He sounded Recall. He sounded it again, and again, while Harman and the other officers raised their field glasses.

Below them, around the lip of the Punchbowl, there was confusion. Men were looking back toward the height. They were wondering what was up. Harman could see Major Darcy gesturing to them, telling them to ignore the bugle call and advance.

The trumpeter kept playing.

Around the Punchbowl, the gunfire slackened. Soldiers started moving back from the rim. They were confused. Men were looking toward Darcy. The firing had almost stopped now. Darcy was ordering them to go forward. The officers were protesting. The men didn't know what to do. The bugle kept playing. The attack had died. Frustrated, Darcy waved an arm, and the men started for their horses. They mounted, formed ranks and started back, bringing as many of the wounded as they could. The remnants of the Pine City Volunteers followed in a bunch.

Major Darcy galloped his black charger ahead of the rest, toward the heights. Even at this distance, the rage was plain on his face.

"Sergeant of the guard," Captain Harman said.

"Serr?" said a big Irish sergeant.

"Detail four men. When I give the word, you are to arrest Major Darcy. If he resists, you are to shoot him. That is an order, sergeant."

"Serr, Oi'll need that in writing, serr."

"You'll have it," said the captain. He scribbled with his pencil in a notebook, tore off a page and handed it to the sergeant. The sergeant read it, saluted and told off his detail.

Major Darcy boiled up the height. At the crest, he reined in his horse angrily. To Harman, he said, "Captain, what the devil is the meaning of this?" He saw Torn and Penny. "What are that Sesesh judge and his whore doing here? I'm warning you, Captain, this had better be good."

"It is good, sir. Sergeant, you may place the major under arrest now."

Darcy exploded. "Ignore that order, sergeant."

The sergeant hesitated, from force of habit. Darcy said, "Are you that gullible, Captain, that you've let these two incite you to mutiny?"

Unlike Darcy's anger, Harman's anger was cold. "Not mutiny, sir. Murder. I'm placing you under

arrest for the murder of Lt. McIntyre and his detail."
There were gasps from the men who had not heard
Torn speak, and Harman went on. "Also for graft,
and for attempting to break a Federal treaty. A formal list of charges will be presented to you before
your court martial."

Darcy turned. "This is all your doing, Torn. These
are more of your lies."

"No, Major, the lies were yours," Clay said. "We
know about the Prometheus Company. We know
how you and Larrabee tried to starve the Indians.
We know how you and Murtaugh dressed white men
as Indians and ran off the ranchers' stock. We know
about the copper deposits in the Red Hills, and we
know how you had Lt. McIntyre killed. Murtaugh
told me everything—just before I shot him."

Darcy paled. Suddenly he wheeled his horse and
tried to get away. Surprised, Harman and the others
stepped back. Torn jumped forward and grabbed the
horse's bridle. The black horse plunged and reared,
but Torn kept his grip. Darcy beat at Torn's arms,
attempting to knock him off.

Then the Irish sergeant recovered. He aimed his
carbine at the major's breast. "Begging the major's
pardon, but that will be enough. Dismount, if ye
playse, serr, or Oi'll fire. Oi had a good friend with
Lt. McIntyre's section, serr. Oi won't miss."

Darcy gave in with good grace. "Very well." To
Harman, he said, "You'll regret this, Captain. You've
destroyed your career by turning on a brother officer."

"The career wasn't worth having if it meant having
to protect a man like you, Major."

Darcy straightened his expensive uniform. He reassumed his air of superiority. "I'll see you in court, sir."

"Yes, sir. No doubt you will, sir," Harman said.

Darcy looked at Torn. "And you, sir. I'll see you in hell."

"Worse luck for you, if you do," Torn told him.

"Take him away," Harman told the sergeant. Major Darcy dismounted. The sergeant and the four guards led him off. Another soldier followed with the major's black charger.

Harman said, "Dr. Rickman. Take your assistant. See to the wounded on both sides. Take a flag of truce, so there will be no mistaking your intentions."

The doctor and his assistant rode off the height, carrying a white flag. As they did, Torn mounted his horse.

"Where are you going?" Captain Harman asked him.

"To the Punchbowl. To see Standing Deer."

CHAPTER

19

TORN RODE OFF THE HEIGHT, TOWARD THE Devil's Punchbowl.

"Wait!" cried a voice. It was Penny. She had re-mounted, and she was coming after him.

"I'll go with you," she said, when she caught up. "I'd like to be what help I can."

"You sure you want to see this?" Torn said.

"No, I don't want to see it. But I've seen war before, and I want to help."

As they approached the battlefield, they saw the doctor and his assistant moving among the dead and wounded soldiers, under a white flag. Standing Deer was old enough and wise enough, and he'd fought the whites enough, to know what a white flag meant, and to respect it. The lightly wounded had been brought off by the retreating attackers. The doctor and his assistant were helping those who required immediate attention. Others were being tagged for secondary attention and operations. Still others they could do nothing for, and those men would wait until last. The gentlemen of the press—and God only knew where they'd been keeping themselves—were already wandering around, taking notes but making no attempt to help the wounded.

Torn and Penny heard the cries of stricken men and animals. They heard men crying for water, men crying for their mothers. They smelled blood and vomit amid the low-lying, acrid swirls of powder smoke. There was no smell of death. Not yet.

Their horses splashed through mud streaked red with blood. They saw men with stomach and chest wounds, covered with mud, certain to be infected. Other men had smashed arms or legs. They were numb now, and they felt little pain. They were cheerful enough, but Torn knew they faced amputation, and futures as cripples and beggars. Men were already stiffening in death, some in strange attitudes. One was on his knees, as if about to fire a rifle. Another was reaching skyward for something. Here and there, horses lay, kicking feebly. Another horse was limping on a shattered foreleg, looking stupidly around him, as if he couldn't understand what had happened to him, or why. In one area, a group of Pine City Volunteers had fallen in a bunch. Torn saw smashed faces and gaping wounds, and wondered if their fate had been worth the forty dollars a week they had been paid.

"I must have seen a hundred battlefields," he told

Penny uneasily, "but I can never get used to it. I can never get used to the waste, the cruelty, the stupidity of war. It makes me sick. It makes me ashamed to be part of the human race." He sighed. "That's one reason I went into the law—to prevent this sort of thing from happening. To try and make a difference. I failed this time, though, and I don't feel good about it."

"But you have made a difference," Penny said. "You've kept this from being much worse than it could have been."

"Tell that to these kids," Torn said bitterly. "Tell it to their families."

He thought about Darcy, the man who had been responsible for all of this. He wished it wasn't left to military justice to punish him. He wished that justice could be more swift, more certain.

Penny saw how black his mood had gotten. "I'll go help the doctor now," she said. She wheeled her horse, and joined the grateful medical men.

Torn rode on into the Punchbowl. The painted Cheyenne warriors watched him warily. Despite the cold, most wore no more than a breechclout. Here and there he saw dead ones, and was struck by how much, in death, they looked like the whites. In the end, they were all men. The corpses were tended by the women, singing their death songs. At the bottom of the depression, a few horses were down, hit by stray bullets.

The Indian casualties were far less than those of the whites, yet they were a beaten people. They were starved and exhausted. Their once proud, fiercely independent spirit was gone, dulled, and

Torn knew it could never be recaptured. He knew they would be beaten down still more in the months and years ahead, and there was nothing anyone could do about it. All the good intentions in the world wouldn't change what the future held for these people.

The price of civilization, Torn thought.

He picked his way across the slope to Standing Deer, who stood out in his magnificent war bonnet. He carried his red shield with the eagle feathers; his face was painted red and yellow. He carried an old Sharps rifle with brass tacks hammered into the butt to make a decoration, and there was a pistol in his waistband. Despite the stand he had just made against the army, or maybe because of it, he looked more than ever like a tired old man. Torn got the impression that he felt that way, too.

Next to Standing Deer was his son, Runs With the Wind, with three eagle feathers in his braided hair and black circles painted around his eyes. Blood dripped down the young man's chest from a wound in his shoulder, but he appeared not to notice. He and his father were standing over a third figure, on the ground. Torn recognized Gray Thunder, the old chief's son-in-law, who had confronted him and Captain Harman that day in the Indian camp. Gray Thunder had been shot in the chest. He was breathing his last, biting his lip to keep from crying out in pain. There was a sucking sound from the wound. Bloody froth bubbled at the corners of his mouth. A young woman was wailing nearby and cutting off her long hair. That must be Standing Deer's daughter, Tall Woman, Gray Thunder's wife, Torn thought. As he watched, the young woman laid her hand on a rock. She drew a knife from the sheath at her waist, and she hacked off the tip of her little finger. Torn wanted to stop her, but it was the Cheyenne way of mourning, and he could not interfere. She might take off three or four of her fingertips before she was through. Her mother was there to take care of her.

Torn dismounted and faced Standing Deer. "I'm sorry," he told the old Indian. "I tried to prevent this."

Standing Deer looked at his dying son-in-law. He spoke in his accented English. "Perhaps it is for the best, Claytorn. Gray Thunder died as he wished to have lived, free, and a warrior. It is left for me to lead my people into slavery."

"Not slavery, Standing Deer." The words seemed to stick in Torn's throat, until he had to force them out. They seemed like lies. "The men who were plotting to steal your land have been discovered. They will be punished. There will be no more fighting between our peoples. The war is over. Tomorrow I go to the white man's village. There, I will use the singing wires to send a message to my chief. I will recommend that Captain Harman be named the new Indian agent."

Standing Deer nodded. "It is good."

"Bury your dead," Torn said. "Tend your wounded. We will do the same. Then take your people back to your winter camp and set up your lodges. Beef will be issued to you—the proper amount this time—and grain for your animals. Captain Harman and I will see that timber is provided for you to build winter shelters, and for firewood. Next year—" he glanced at Runs With the Wind— "you will learn to farm, as was promised."

Runs With the Wind looked pleased, but Standing Deer said, "It is well that you do this, Claytorn, but still my heart is heavy. We will never again see the old ways."

"We cannot undo what is done, Standing Deer. We can only go on, and try to make things better."

The old chief looked into Torn's eyes with his searching, forceful gaze. "Will things get better?"

Torn hesitated. How could he tell the truth? How could he explain to these primitive nomads that they were victims of history? They had no concept of history. They knew only the seasons, and the land, and the spirits who ruled over all. He said, "I must speak true. I do not know what the future holds for you or your people. I can only promise good intentions and honesty on the part of the white man— this time. More than that, I cannot say."

"We must hope, Father," Runs With the Wind said. "Without hope there is no life."

From the height above the Punchbowl came a scattering of gunshots.

Torn turned instinctively, even though he could see nothing from here. "What is that?"

"Perhaps they are killing wounded horses," Runs With the Wind suggested.

"No," Torn said. "Not up there. There were no wounded horses there." An uneasy feeling came over him. "I'd better get back," he said.

Torn swung onto his horse. He rode out of the Punchbowl. Penny and the doctor were working on the Indian wounded now, bandaging them, giving them water. Penny was staring toward the sound of the shots, and she looked at Torn questioningly as he rode by.

Torn left the Punchbowl. He rode carefully across the battlefield, picking his way among the dead and wounded. Past the battlefield, he spurred his horse into a gallop and made his way up the height.

At the top, he found the soldiers in a state of confusion. A knot of officers was gathered around Captain Harman. He was sitting on a boulder, wincing and cursing under his breath, while subordinates looked on solicitously. He had been shot in the foot.

"What happened?" Torn asked.

"It's Darcy," Harman said. "He's escaped."

CHAPTER 20

THE IRISH SERGEANT STOOD OFF TO ONE SIDE looking downcast and guilty.

"It was my fault," Captain Harman told Torn bitterly. "Darcy gave his word of honor that if we didn't put him under restraint, he wouldn't try anything. He's a West Pointer, and I was stupid enough to believe that his word of honor meant something to him. Next thing I knew, he'd pulled a gun from somewhere, got his horse and shot his way out. I tried to stop him, and he got me in the foot."

Harman looked around, "Captain Yates. Take the first two sections of K Company. Prepare to follow Major Darcy and bring him back. Rations for ten days."

"Yes, sir," said Yates.

To Harman, Torn said, "Excuse me, Captain, but no detail is going to catch Darcy on that horse of his. This is a job for one man. A man who can travel fast and light."

"You seem to be nominating yourself," Harman said.

"I am."

"This is a military matter, Judge. You've no brief here."

Torn's eyes narrowed. His voice was harsh. "Darcy—" he refused to call him Major, anymore "—had his own men murdered. He betrayed his honor as a soldier. I lived by that honor for four years. I reckon I've got as much right to go after him as anybody."

Harman thought for a moment. "Very well. Captain Yates and his men will follow you to bring back the prisoner."

Torn smiled grimly, but didn't say anything. "Which is the best horse here, after Darcy's? The animal I took from Murtaugh's men has been ridden hard for two days, and he's tired."

"Take mine, if you can ride him," Harman said. "He's called Cossack."

Harman motioned, and his soldier striker led up the horse, a chestnut gelding with a blaze forehead. Full grain bags were put on the animals' saddle. For himself, Torn took soldiers' rations—salt pork and hard biscuit. "You should all win the Medal of Honor, for eating this stuff," he cracked, and the soldiers laughed.

Torn gathered the reins and mounted. The horse bucked a bit under the unfamiliar rein, but Torn steadied him. Behind him, Yates and his detail were getting ready. Below the height, the doctor and Penny were still moving among the wounded. Others were helping now, too. A mule loaded with medical supplies was being led down to them. Penny didn't see Torn go. She was too busy.

"Good luck," Harman said. His boot was off, and one of the soldiers was bandaging his foot.

Torn nodded. "Thanks."

He rode back through the Red Hills. There was no point trying to pick out Darcy's tracks in the churned-up ground. He maintained as steady a pace as he could on the rough terrain.

He left the Red Hills and came onto the prairie. There he stopped. Which way would Darcy go?

East? No. That was the first direction anyone would look. Besides, he'd have to travel east a long way before he came to a town of any size. Northwest, then, along the Bozeman Trail to the Montana mining settlements? It was like the end of the world up there. A man could lose himself and no questions asked. Darcy could winter over and then travel to California. It would be a long ride through Sioux country, but nobody said Darcy didn't have guts.

The possibility was appealing, but Torn decided against it. Murtaugh had said that Darcy had a big-spending wife. He'd want to go someplace close, or as close as it got out here. Someplace he could send for his wife and spend the winter in relative comfort.

Denver, Torn decided. A man with money could live well in Denver, and since Darcy had thought of everything else, Torn was sure he had some of Murtaugh's money with him. That, or he'd have his wife bring it.

Between the melted snow and the passing of Indians and soldiers, the ground hereabouts was so cut up that God himself couldn't have found Darcy's tracks. Torn cut a wide half-circle to the south and west. After a while, he found the tracks of a single rider, moving fast. He smiled to himself.

The sun was low. Night would be coming on soon. Torn checked the sky. It looked clear, but you couldn't tell, this time of year. They could be under four feet of snow by tomorrow. He took a swig from his canteen and started off at a steady lope.

Darcy was no fool. He wouldn't put on a burst of speed then let up, feeling himself safe from pursuit. He'd ride through the night, putting as many miles between himself and the army as he could. After that, with his advantage in horseflesh, and the fact that any pursuing detail would have to keep the pace of the slowest mount, he'd be able to take his time. Torn didn't expect to catch him today, or even tomorrow. Tornorrow evening, maybe, as he went into camp. Somewhere along the breaks of the Niobrara.

Torn rode the rest of the afternoon and into the evening. Darcy's trail was easy to follow on the broad, undulating prairie. Periodically, Torn rested the chestnut and watered him, then re-mounted and kept going.

The sun set. Darcy's tracks bore steadily south and west. He had not tried to hide them. Once he got to Denver, he could change his identity and hope the army would never find him.

Into the darkness Torn rode. The big chestnut ate

up the miles without protest. The horse didn't have blinding speed, but he could keep up this pace a long time. The wind blew cold from the northwest, and Torn buttoned the coat he had taken from Van Horne. Overhead, millions of stars sparkled in frosty grandeur. The immensity of their setting dwarfed the puny strivings of those on earth. A shooting star trailed across the heavens.

Sometime after midnight Torn camped by a shallow stream. He let the horse rest, and wrapped himself in his blankets. He was up again before dawn, built a fire in the numbing cold and made coffee. He grained and watered the horse, then fried a bit of the salt pork. He smashed the hard biscuit with his pistol butt and mushed it in with the pork, then sprinkled the mixture with brown sugar and ate it, washing it down with more coffee. Then he saddled the horse and rode off again, as the first trace of light crept into the eastern sky.

He did not find Darcy's tracks right away, and for a while he was worried that the ex-soldier had tricked him and turned in another direction. But it was only natural that the two men had diverged in the darkness, and casting a loop westward, he soon came upon the trail again.

The sun crept higher in the sky. It grew warm enough to take off the heavy coat, which Torn did gratefully. He hated wearing anything that had been on the back of a man like Cornelius Van Horne.

It was nearly noon when Torn spied something on the prairie ahead. Something lying in a lump, with a horse nearby. A dead man.

Torn reined in the gelding and searched the horizon. There was no sign of Indians, no sign of anyone.

He drew his revolver, the one he'd taken from Gallagher, and rode toward the dead man cautiously. The man's horse shied away as Torn came up. The dead man lay on his back, wearing only his underwear. He was a young man, with several days' growth of beard, a cowboy, as evidenced by the high-heeled boots discarded nearby. He'd been shot in the back of the head, his brains blown out the front. Torn had no idea what he'd been doing out here. Heading to or from Ogallala, likely.

Darcy must have come upon the cowboy, pretended to befriend him, then murdered him and taken his clothes. The poor waddie would never have expected trouble from a major of the famous Seventh Cavalry. Darcy's army saddle was lying near the body, so he had switched saddles as well as clothes. He had changed identities. He must be laughing to himself.

Torn buried the cowboy. He snubbed a lead line to his saddle and took the dead man's horse with him. There was no sense leaving the animal out here for the wolves. He mounted the chestnut and started riding.

Torn's sense of anticipation grew as the afternoon wore on. He was not far behind his quarry now. He could feel it. Darcy's tracks were fresher. He had slowed. He must believe that he'd put enough distance between himself and the pursuit, that he could take it easy the rest of the way into Denver. Torn crossed the White River. At this point, the Niobrara was not far.

At dusk, Torn topped a low ridge, and saw the breaks of the Niobrara in the distance.

As darkness descended, he approached the bluffs. Below him, he saw a pinpoint of light.

CHAPTER 21

IT WAS DAWN. STEPHEN DARCY WAS CAMPED on an island in the middle of the Niobrara. There was water in the river from the melting snow, and it ran over the rocky bottom with a rushing sound. The island was thick with cottonwoods. It provided shelter from wind and storm. On either side of the river, bluffs rose precipitously.

Darcy was finishing a leisurely breakfast. He had shaved off his moustache, and had a day's growth of beard. His new face felt strange, but he supposed he'd get used to it. He wore his army greatcoat against the morning cold, over the dead cowboy's clothing. The cowboy's greasy hat was over one eye. His own gleaming boots stuck out from under the dead man's chaps and blue jeans. The cowboy's boots

173

had not fit Darcy, and anyway, he had not wanted to give up his own boots, he'd spent too long breaking them in. By the time he reached Denver, they'd be scuffed enough that they wouldn't attract attention. He reached inside the cowboy's flannel shirt and scratched his armpit. The cowboy had had lice or fleas, or both. Boorish fellow.

Darcy fed and watered his black horse and saddled him. He felt no sense of haste. He was far ahead of any detail that Harman could send after him. Three days should see him in Denver. His military career was over, but there were other possibilities, once his wife joined him with the money he'd gotten from Murtaugh. It wasn't anywhere near as much money as he would have earned had the plan gone through, but it would keep the wolves from the door until he could think of a way to earn more.

He gathered the horse's reins and prepared to mount. Then he stopped.

Across the stream, at the water's edge, stood a man. It was Clay Torn.

Torn cradled the Winchester casually. "Morning, Darcy."

"How . . . how did you get here?" Darcy stammered. "I never heard you."

"That was the idea," Torn told him.

"How long have you been there?"

"All night."

Darcy paled. "You could have killed me in my sleep."

"I thought about it," Torn said. "It would have been enjoyable, but it's not the way I work. That's for folks like you."

Darcy recovered his composure. A smile crossed his stubbled lips. "I commend your persistence, Judge. You've come to take me back, I suppose?"

"Nope," Torn said. "Taking you back isn't what I planned. I like my justice certain. The idea of delivering you to a court martial, where a jury of your West Point friends might let you go with a slap on the wrist, doesn't appeal to me—especially since all the direct witnesses against you are dead."

Darcy understood. He said, "Are you going to give me a chance?"

"More of a chance than you gave poor McIntyre and his boys. Now, make your move."

For a moment, the only sound was the rushing of water across rocks. Then Darcy pushed the horse away, at the same time pulling his rifle from the saddle bucket.

Torn leveled the Winchester. He hesitated. He didn't want to hit the horse. As the horse dashed by, Darcy dropped to cover at the edge of the stream. He fired at Torn. Torn fired back. The crack of the rifles was loud in the river bottom. Darcy fired again. He stood and ran back on the island, into a stand of leafless cottonwoods. Torn sprinted across the stream after him. The icy water numbed his feet and ankles. Darcy fired; the bullet hummed by his face. Torn snapped a shot with the Winchester and dropped to the ground behind a fold of earth.

He wiggled forward, but couldn't see much at this level; trees and brush hid his view. The rustle of dead leaves gave him away, but he couldn't help it. He raised his head cautiously. There was the loud crack of the Sharps. The bullet hit in front of him, kicking cold mud into his eyes.

Torn clawed the mud from his eyes, then he rolled, got up and ran forward. He fired once with the Winchester, to keep Darcy's head down. He wove through the trees, toward Darcy's last position, and crouched behind a large tree, looking around carefully, trying to hear above the loudness of his own breathing. There was nothing.

Darcy's horse was across the stream, cropping the brown autumn grass. If Darcy made for the animal, he would be an easy target. The island was small—he had to be close. Torn waited, trusting Darcy to lose his nerve.

Suddenly Darcy bounded to his feet, not more than twenty yards away, and dashed for the far side of the island. Torn stood and fired. The Winchester jammed. Torn worked the lever furiously. The rifle jammed again. Torn swore. These repeaters had a delicate mechanism. Either Gallagher had never cleaned it, or Torn had fouled it crawling across the island. Probably both. He threw the rifle down and started after Darcy with his pistol. He was at a serious disadvantage now. Darcy's Sharps was accurate to a mile; the revolver wasn't accurate at much past point-blank range.

Darcy splashed across the stream and disappeared into a belt of trees at the foot of the bluffs. Torn would have to get close to him somehow. He took a breath and launched himself from behind the tree. He ran toward Darcy's left, cursing his limp. The limp only slowed him a half-step, but a half-step was all a good marksman needed. He splashed into the water, praying it wouldn't be deep enough to slow him. He saw Darcy rise from the trees. Both men fired at the same time. There was no telling where the bullets went. Torn's heart was pounding. He fired again, then he was across the stream, and he dove for cover. There was a rifle shot, and a bullet screamed off a nearby rock.

Torn rolled right. He crawled forward, through a low depression, trying not to make noise. Darcy was up and running again, toward the rocky bluffs. Torn fired the pistol at him, saw him drop but knew he hadn't hit him, not at this distance. Torn continued working to the right. He wanted to get above the rocks. There was a shot. The bullet hit near Torn's last position.

"Where are you, Judge?" taunted Darcy.

Torn saw Darcy move further up the bluffs, where he had a good view of the approaches. Torn kept crawling to Darcy's right.

"Torn? Are you still alive?"

A jagged ravine ran down the side of the bluffs. Torn worked himself into it, hauling himself up, foot by foot, testing each handhold and footrest. It was quiet in the river bottom. A few birds called. Gusts of breeze rattled the leafless trees. Torn's legs and feet were freezing from the water. He tried to keep his teeth from chattering as he climbed.

There was a wild shot down the hill. Darcy yelled, "Come on out, Torn. What's the matter? You afraid?"

At last, Torn reached a spot above Darcy. A rock ledge ran roughly toward Darcy's position, and he followed it. Quietly. He put the pistol in its holster.

Below him, Darcy was still looking down the bluffs, fingering his rifle nervously. "Come on, Sesesh!"

Torn worked his way along the ledge. His feet were frozen, and it was hard to place them. His leg hurt, and he tried to ignore it. He was close to Darcy now. A little bit more, and he'd be able to use the pistol.

His foot dislodged a rock. The rock bounced down the bluff side.

Darcy returned and saw Torn. He raised his rifle. Torn ran forward. He leaped.

He landed on Darcy before Darcy could fire. The two men tumbled down the bluff in a welter of dirt and mud, cutting themselves on the rocks, tearing their clothes.

They stopped rolling near the bottom, and came to their feet slowly, breathing hard, shaking off waves of pain. Darcy reached for his pistol. Torn did the same, but the weapon had spilled out of its holster in the fall down the hill.

Torn threw himself forward. He caught Darcy's gun hand in both his own, just as Darcy fired. The bullet went wide. The powder blast scorched the side of Torn's face. The two men wrestled for the pistol. Torn tried to make Darcy drop it. Darcy smashed Torn's face with his free hand. He clawed at Torn's eyes. Torn bent Darcy's gun wrist, trying to break it. Darcy yelled with pain and dropped the pistol. At the same time he hooked a leg behind Torn and the two men fell to the cold mud.

They rolled around, punching, scratching, grunting with their efforts, each trying to get an advantage. Then Darcy saw an opening, and he drove a knee into Torn's groin. Torn lost his grip. Bile rose in his throat. There was a film before his eyes.

Darcy rolled away. He crawled to his feet. He pulled a bowie knife from his belt, moved in, and slashed at Torn, who managed to scramble out of the way. Torn struggled to his feet. Before Darcy could move in again, Torn reached behind his back and pulled out his saber-knife.

The two men circled each other, heaving for air. There were covered with mud, bleeding from numerous cuts. Darcy feinted, and Torn moved back. "I was fencing champion at the Academy, you know," Darcy said.

"This isn't the Academy," Torn replied.

Darcy lunged. Torn turned the blow aside. Their blades clanged. Again Darcy lunged. Again Torn parried. Metal rang against metal in the silence of the river bottom.

"No pretend Indians to do your dirty work this time, are there?" Torn asked.

"I don't need help to kill a Sesesh like you."

Darcy launched an all-out attack, slashing, lunging, his face contorted with rage. Torn skipped backward, dodging the razor-sharp metal, waiting for an opening. Then Torn's leg got twisted in a hole and he went down, catching himself on one hand. He looked up as Darcy lunged forward, eyes alight, chopping with the long blade. Torn dodged to one side and raised his own blade, letting Darcy run up onto it, burying it to the hilt in Darcy's breast.

Torn let go of the saber's hilt. Darcy's momentum carried him on a few steps. Then he stumbled and slumped to his knees.

Torn rose. He limped over slowly. Darcy looked up at him, the life fading rapidly from his eyes. He vomited blood from his nose and mouth.

Torn stared Darcy in the eye. He spoke while Darcy could still grasp the meaning of the words. "Now you've seen a man killed by a sword," he said.

He pulled out the blade. Blood gushed from Darcy's chest. Darcy held Torn's gaze for a moment, then toppled onto his face.

CHAPTER 22

PENELOPE WINSLOW CAME OUT OF THE TEL-
egraph office, where she had filed her dispatch on
the battle of the Devil's Punchbowl and its aftermath.
Behind her, other reporters lined up, waiting their
turns. Torn was waiting for Penny out front. They
were both cleaned and scrubbed. Penny wore a pow-
der-blue riding dress, with violet facings. Torn had
on his old buckskin jacket. The powder burn on
Torn's cheek where Darcy had almost shot him was
still visible. Two saddled horses were tied nearby.

The street was snarled with traffic. Pine City was
emptying. Men were pulling up their tents and heading elsewhere. There was no use staying. The few
frame buildings were abandoned, as was the crated
machinery in the Prometheus lot. The road out of

town was choked with wagons, horsemen, and men on foot, carrying their belongings in carpetbags or in sacks slung over poles. The only working structure left in town was the telegraph office, and when the reporters were done, the telegraph would move to Fort Connor.

"It's amazing," Penny said. "In a few days there won't be anything here but the fort."

"Even the fort might not be here long," Torn said. "There's talk of trouble with the Sioux. The Seventh Cavalry might be moving north next year."

Torn and Penny mounted their horses. They rode out of town together.

"It's all over," Penny said. "Murtaugh and Darcy are dead. The Cheyenne will get to keep their land, and Captain Harman has been confirmed as Indian agent."

"And you've got the material for another best-selling book, starring yourself," Torn said, with his easy grin. Then he added, "There's still one piece of unfinished business—Van Horne. When the truth about what he's been doing comes out, I expect his political career will be over."

Penny laughed cynically. "You don't know the ways of Washington, Judge. Congress doesn't like to hear ill of its own, much less take action against them. My guess is, Van Horne will claim to be a victim of Darcy's and Murtaugh's chicanery. The gullible country boy, taken in by city slickers. He'll admit a degree of bad judgment, and the party leaders will close ranks around him. They may even go to the nation for sympathy. Van Horne will probably become chairman of his committee, then run for the Senate. Because of his experience out here, I wouldn't be surprised to see him one day end up as Secretary of the Interior."

It was a sobering thought, and they rode on in silence. Gradually, they distanced themselves from the general exodus. By that afternoon, they had reached the Red Hills reservation boundary, not far from the spot where Torn had met Lt. McIntyre that first day.

They stopped on a low rise to rest their horses. They dismounted, their breaths turning to vapor in the cold. They looked back along the valley. Below them, the stream still sparkled in the sun, but the grass was brown now, and the hardwoods were bare, lending a barren look to the scene.

Suddenly, Penny grabbed Torn's sleeve. "Look," she said.

Torn followed her gaze. On the far spur of a hill was a lone horsemen, watching them. He was a paunchy figure, sitting a scrawny horse, but even at this distance he had a commanding presence. As Torn and Penny looked, the years seemed to drop away from the horseman, until he seemed like a vision from the past.

Penny waved. Torn lifted a hand. The horseman made no response.

Penny turned to Torn. "Will it work out for him and his people?"

Torn took a deep breath. "I don't know. They'll have to keep fighting, but it'll be a different kind of fight, in the courts and on the battlefield of public opinion. One thing is sure—the whites will never stop trying to take this land. It's too valuable. Standing Deer's time is past. It's up to Runs With the Wind and his sons to hold onto the land, now—and up to people like us to help them. Whether we'll be successful, only time will tell."

They looked back to the distant spur, but the horseman was gone, almost as if he had never been there, leaving no mark upon the land.

After a moment, Torn said, "We better go."

He put his hands around Penny's waist to help her into the saddle. She turned in his grip, put her arms around Torn, and kissed him. Her lips were warm and full. Torn's response was halfhearted, but Penny seemed not to notice. As their lips drew apart, she whispered, "You know, Clay, I could get attached to you. Very attached."

"Don't." Torn told her.

Penny lowered her eyes. "It's . . . it's because of my reputation, isn't it?"

Torn smoothed her mane of golden hair. He smelled its honeyed freshness. "No. It's not that."

"Yes, it is. You think I'm a whore." She looked back up at him. "I have a confession to make. I'm a virgin."

Torn stared at her, wide-eyed.

She went on, "The other . . . it's all for publicity, to sell newspapers and books. People buy because there's a breath of scandal. You know, Penny Winslow and the pirate king of Sumatra. Penny Winslow and her jungle porters. Penny Winslow and anything in pants. People want to think they can read the real story between the lines. I don't like it, but it's business."

Torn shook his head. "A girl as beautiful as you.

It's hard to believe you've never had a man."

"Maybe I've never found the right man," she said softly.

Torn pursed his lips. "I'm sorry, Penny, but I can't be that man."

He told her about Melony—how Melony had been taken after the war, and about his long search for her. He showed her the daguerreotype of Melony, one side of its brass frame creased by a bullet.

When he was finished, Penny looked up at him, and her green eyes, though sad, were filled with admiration. "You really are a knight-errant, aren't you?"

"No. I'm just a man, looking for somebody. And someday I'm going to find her."

Penny's eyes misted, though she tried to seem cheerful. "You know what? Someday I believe you will."

Then she laid a hand on his arm. "Clay? Promise me one thing, will you? You won't tell anybody about me. It would ruin my career."

Torn winked. "Your secret's safe," he told her.

He helped her into the saddle. When she was seated, she pointed east, down the valley, "You see that stand of live oaks?"

Torn looked, puzzled, "Yeah. What about them?"

"I'll race you. Five dollars to the winner." She kicked her horse and galloped away.

"Why, you little . . . ," Torn swore, He swung into the saddle and galloped her. Twin plumes of dust mingled as one above their receding figures.